W9-BDV-810

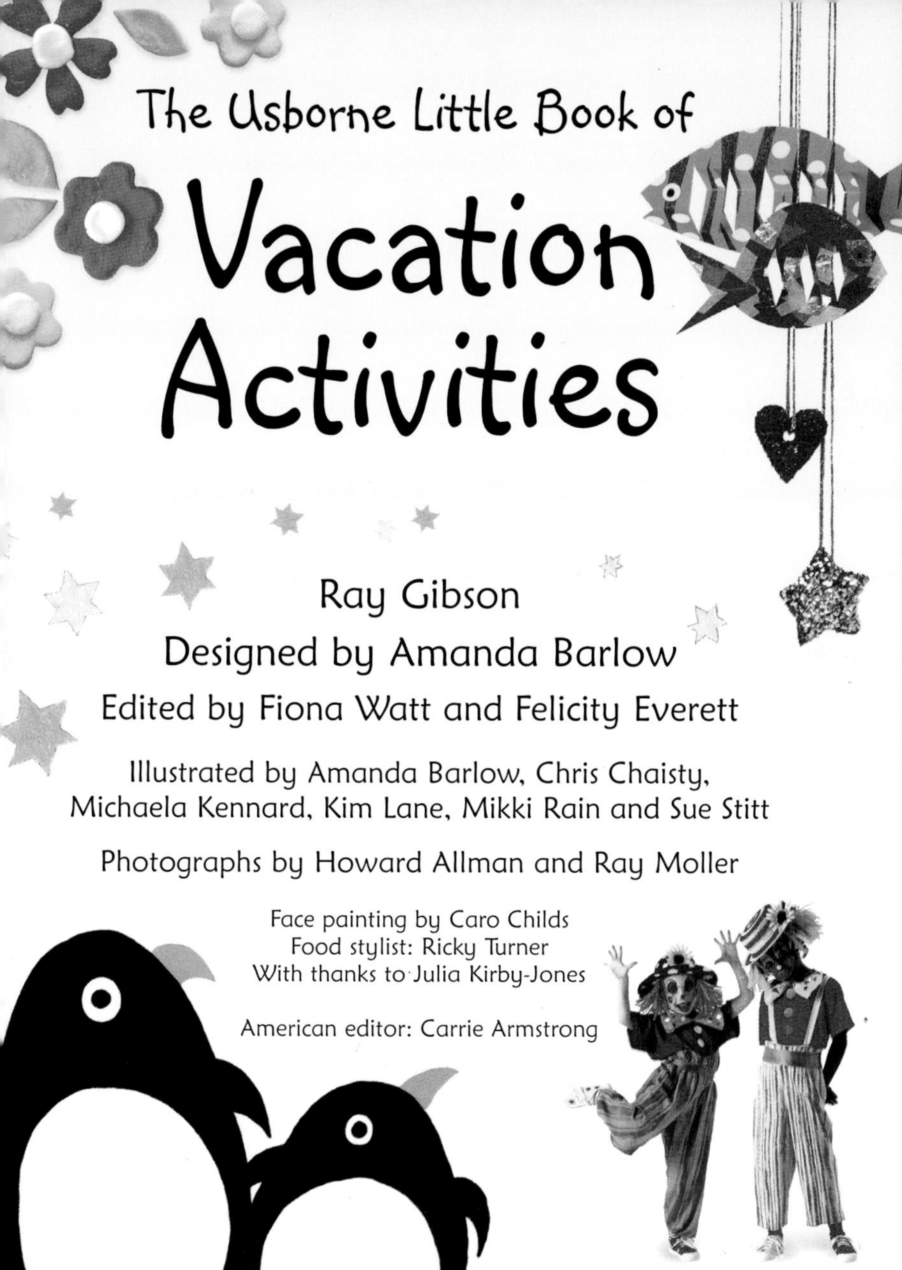

The Usborne Little Book of

Vacation Activities

Ray Gibson

Designed by Amanda Barlow

Edited by Fiona Watt and Felicity Everett

Illustrated by Amanda Barlow, Chris Chaisty, Michaela Kennard, Kim Lane, Mikki Rain and Sue Stitt

Photographs by Howard Allman and Ray Moller

Face painting by Caro Childs
Food stylist: Ricky Turner

With thanks to Julia Kirby-Jones

American editor: Carrie Armstrong

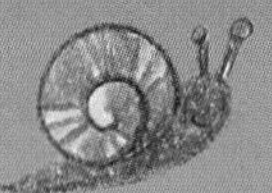

Contents

Drawing

Cooking

Painting

Gardening

Making things

Dressing up

First published in 2005 by Usborne Publishing Ltd, 83-85 Saffron Hill, London EC1N 8RT, England. www.usborne.com

Printed in Dubai. AE. First published in America in 2005.

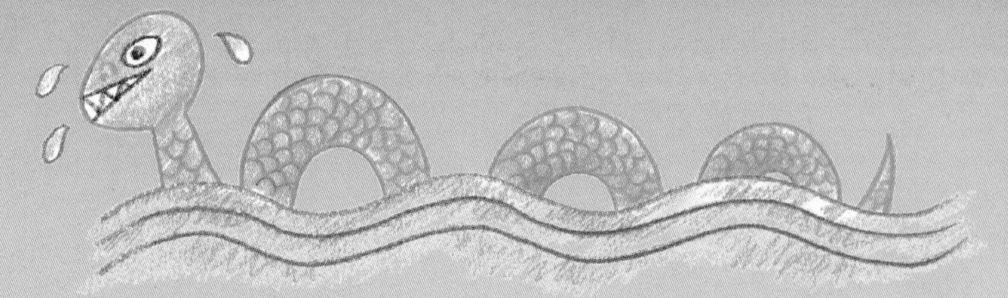

What shall I do today?

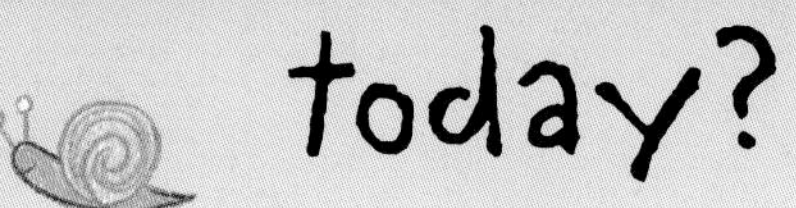

Drawing

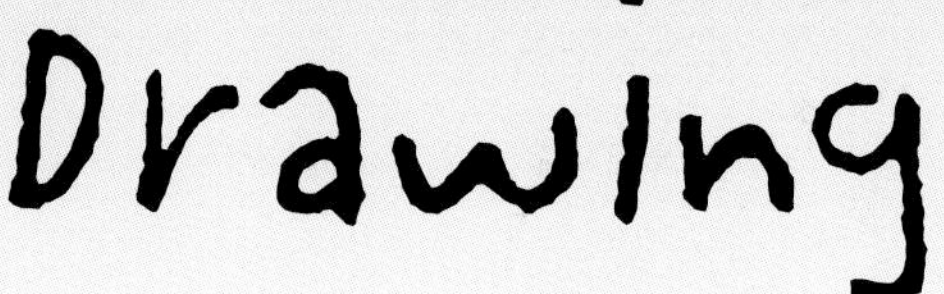

Draw a sea monster

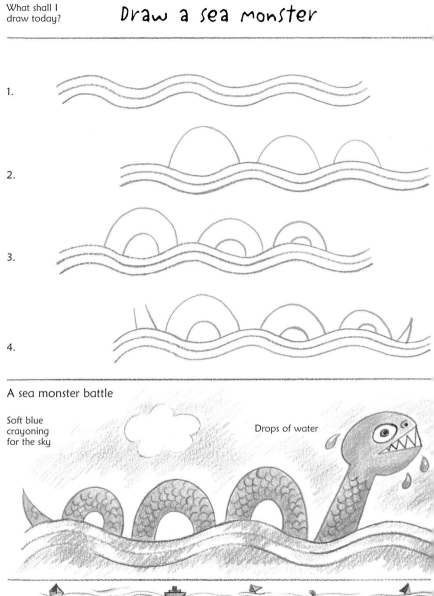

1.

2.

3.

4.

A sea monster battle

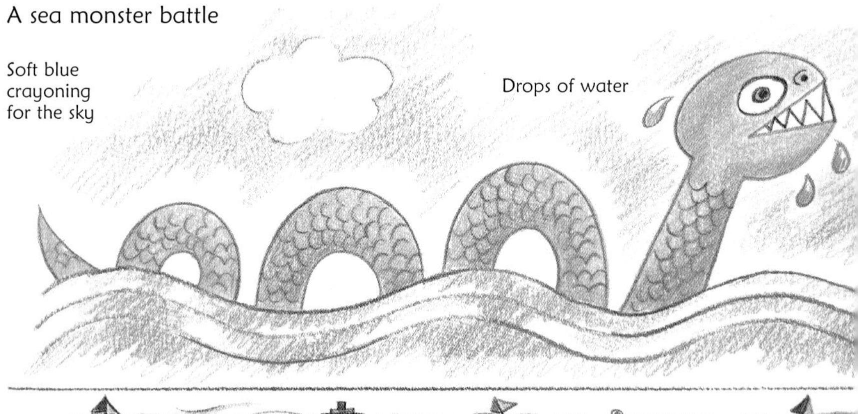

Use a wide sheet of paper.

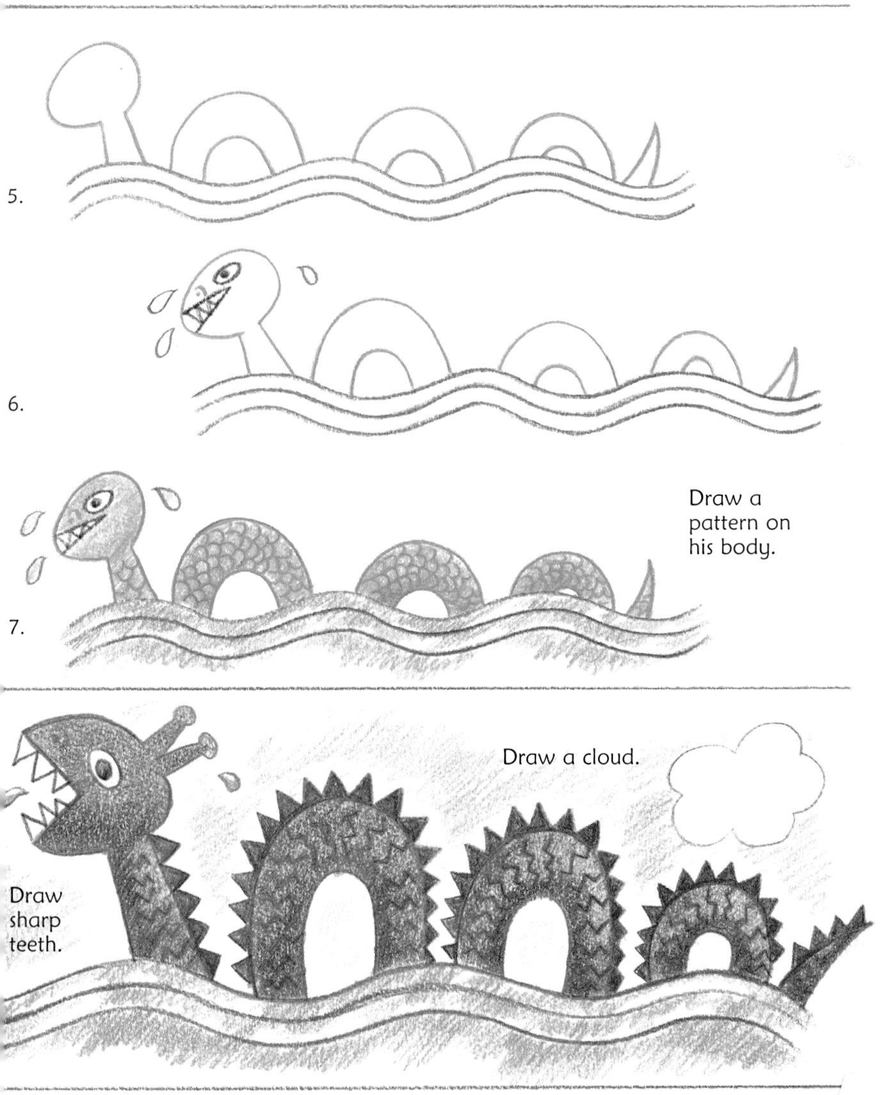

Now how about... a sea monster meeting a boat?

Draw a snail

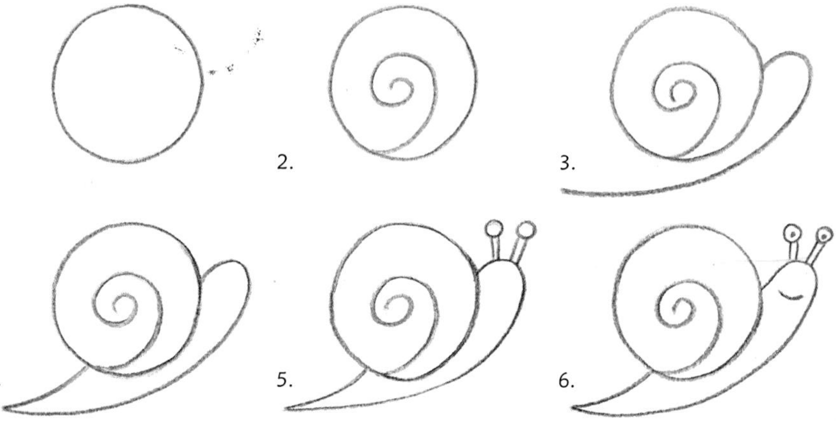

1.

2.

3.

4.

5.

6.

Crayon in the body.

7.

8.

Make a pattern on the shell.

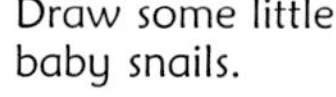

Draw some little baby snails.

Make the shells different.

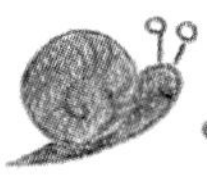

Make a picture story

1.

2.

3.

Draw snails
on a flower.
Add some
grass and
leaves.
Open
mouth
Jagged bite
in the leaf
4.
5.
6.

Now how about... a snail race?

Draw a wizard

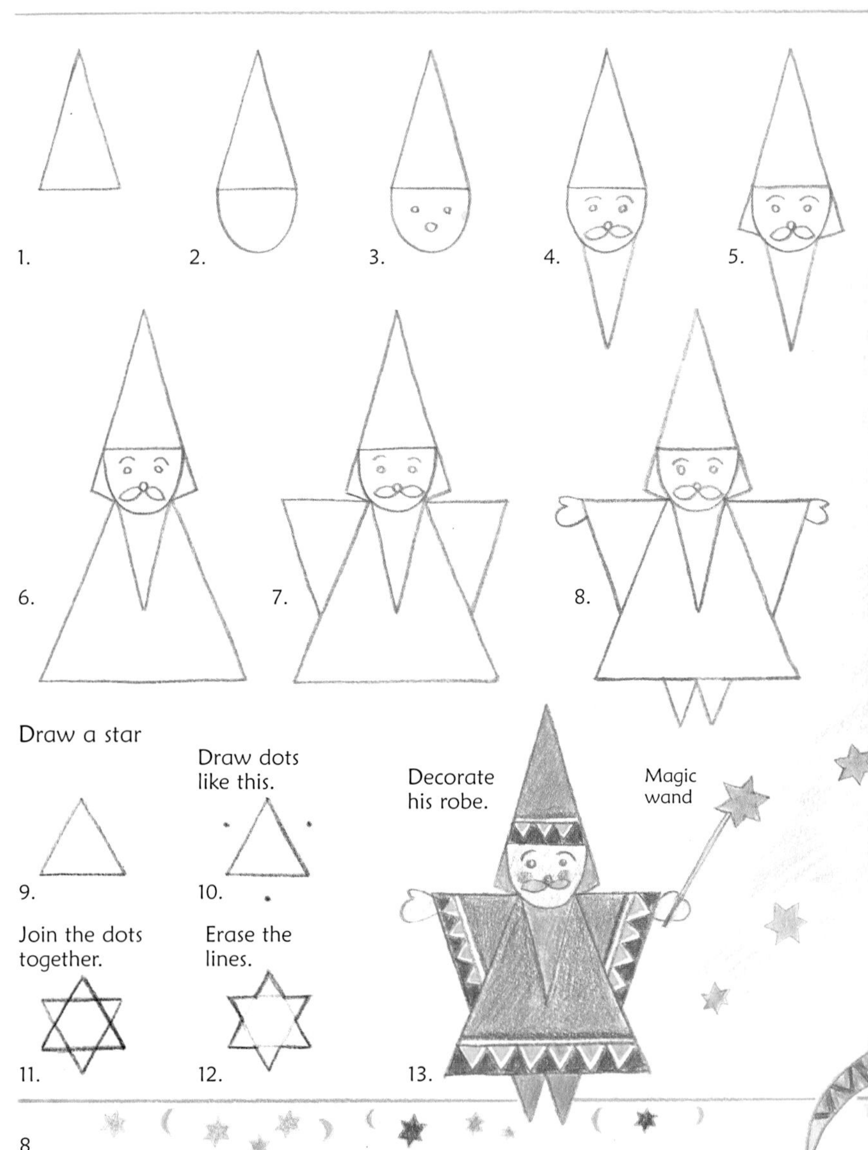

Draw some stars
to show he is
casting a spell.
Spell book
Snake
Cauldron

Now how about... a wizards' party?

Draw a cat

Sleeping cat

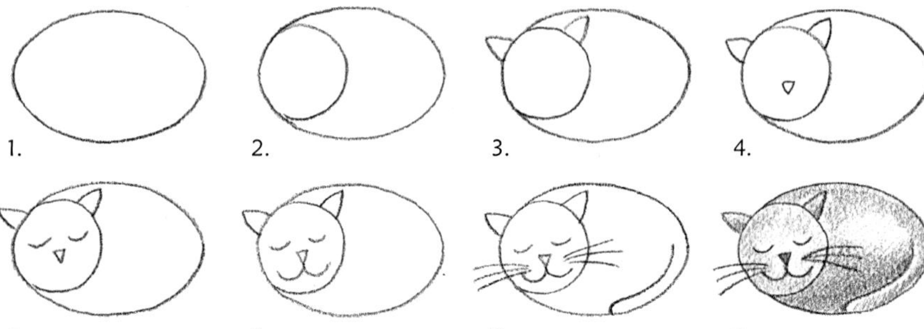

Standing cat

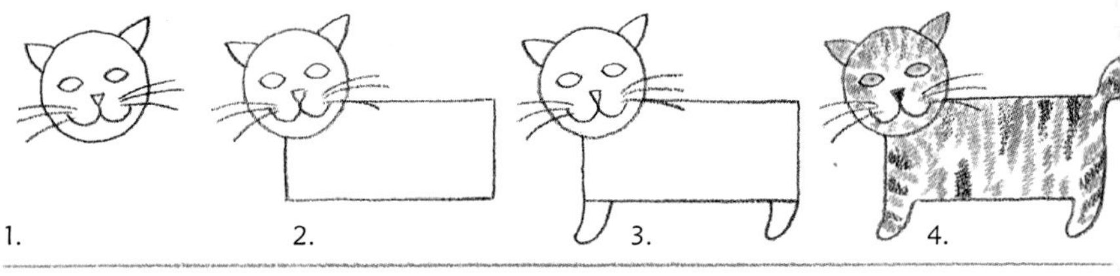

Crouching cat

1. Draw the body in pencil first.

2. Erase one end. Draw in the head.

3.

4.

Lapping cat

Add a tongue and a saucer of milk.

Sitting cat

Cat family

Draw a large sitting cat for the mother.

Comfy cat

Draw the sleeping cat on a cushion.

Now draw the kittens. Add two paws beneath each head.

Don't forget their tails.

Draw a box for the kittens.

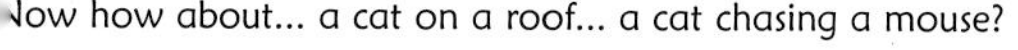

Now how about... a cat on a roof... a cat chasing a mouse?

Draw a clown

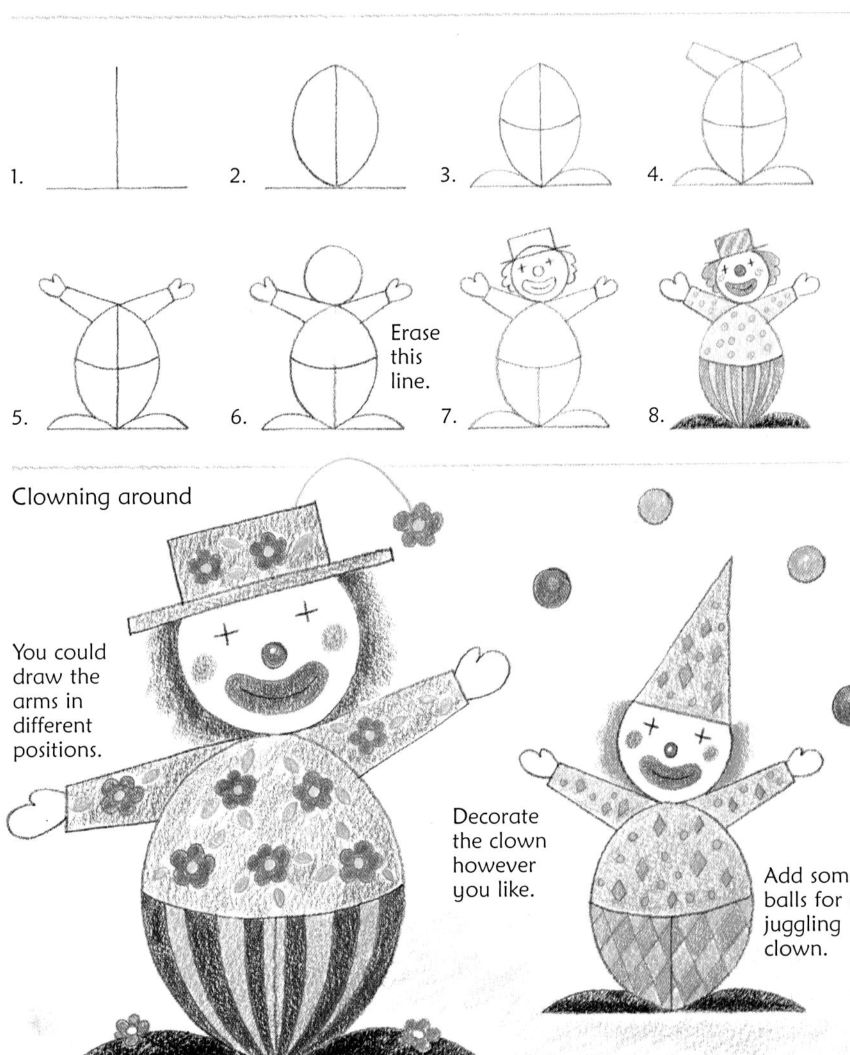
1.
2.
3.
4.
5.
6.
Erase this line.
7.
8.
Clowning around
You could draw the arms in different positions.
Decorate the clown however you like.
Add som
balls for
juggling clown.

Now how about... a circus?

What shall I draw today?

Draw a ballerina

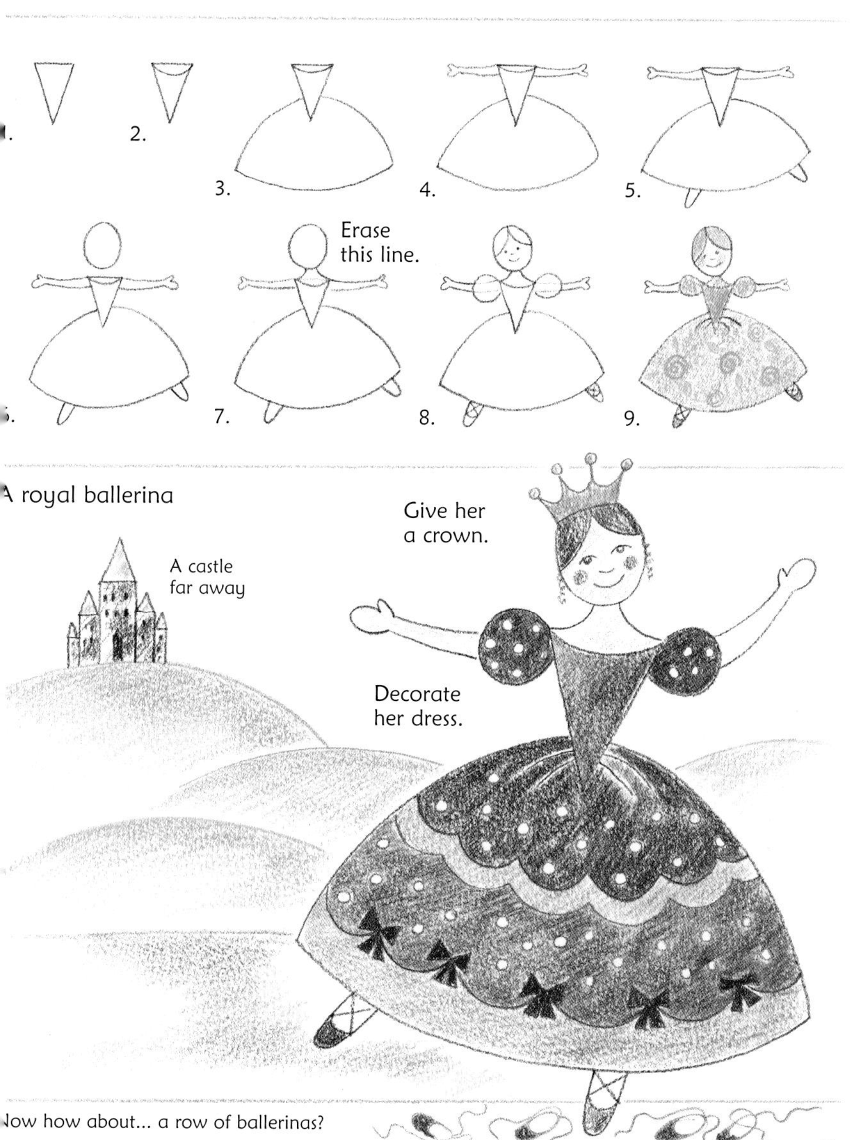

Now how about... a row of ballerinas?

Draw a teddy

1. 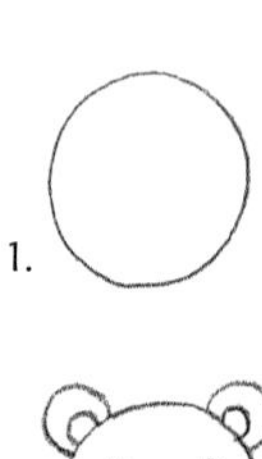

2. 

3. 

4. 

5. 

6. 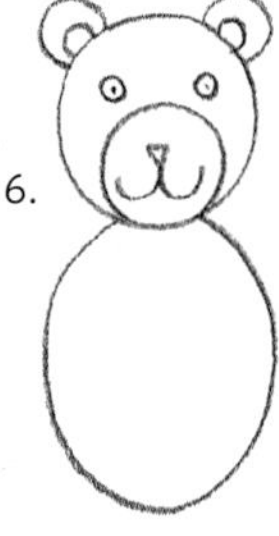

7. 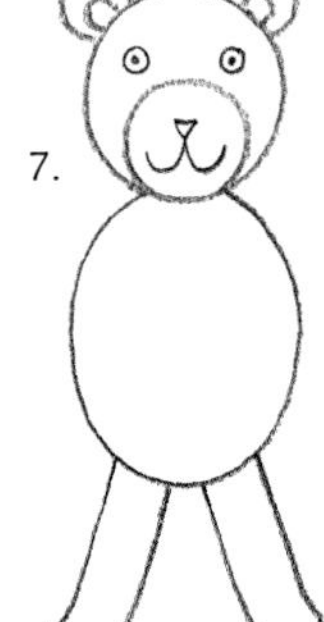

8. 

9. 

Walking Teddy

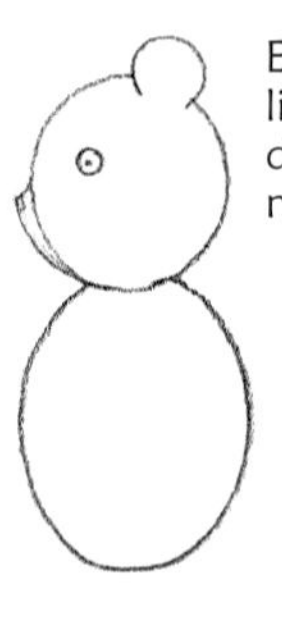

Erase the lines you don't need.

Sitting teddy

Erase the lines you don't need.

Shouting teddy

Draw the mouth open.

Now how about... teddy bears at a swimming pool?

Draw a pick-up truck

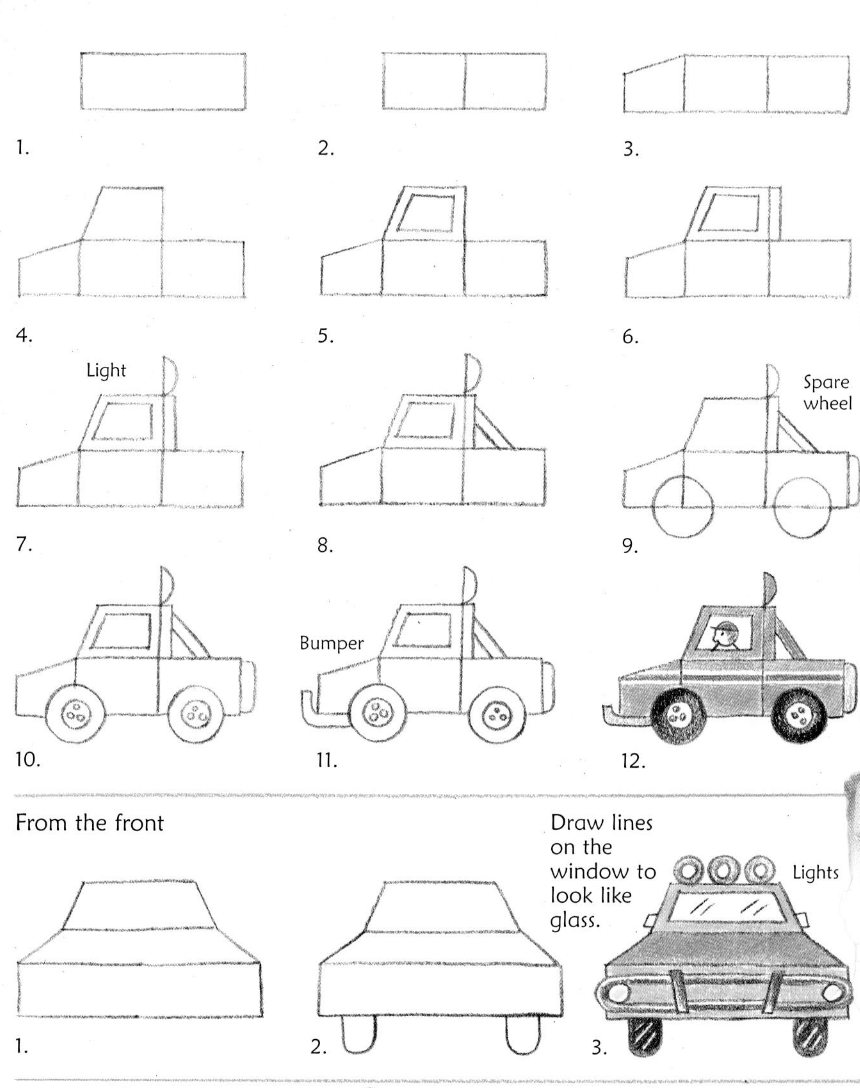

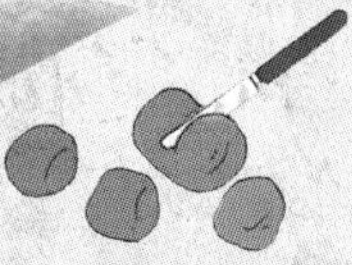

5. Cut the dough in half. Put half into the refrigerator and divide the rest into five pieces.

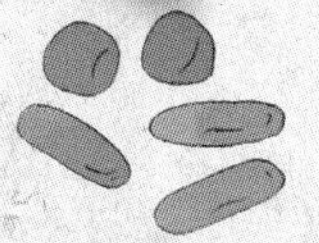

6. Put a little flour on your hands and squeeze and roll the dough into sausage shapes.

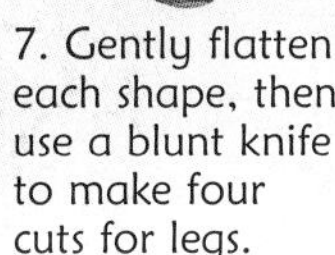

7. Gently flatten each shape, then use a blunt knife to make four cuts for legs.

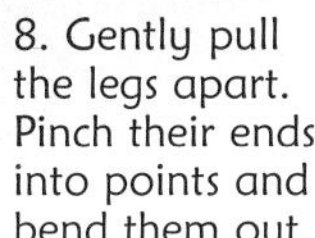

8. Gently pull the legs apart. Pinch their ends into points and bend them out.

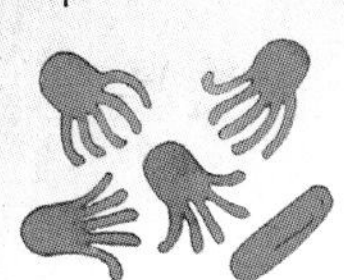

9. Take the other half of dough out of the refrigerator and make five more octopuses.

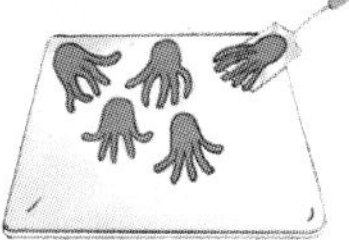

10. Lift the octopuses onto the cookie sheet. Bake them for 10-12 minutes.

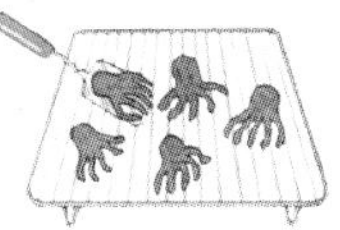

11. Leave them to cool for a little while before putting them on a cooling rack.

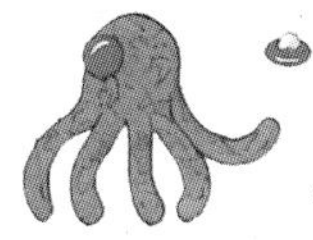

12. Mix the butter and powdered sugar and put it on the candy. Press them on for eyes.

Shining star cookies

For about 24 cookies, you will need:
½ cup brown sugar
⅓ cup soft margarine
half a small beaten egg
1¼ cups flour
1 teaspoon allspice
assorted flavors of hard candy
large cookie cutter
small, round cutter, slightly bigger than the candy
a greased cookie sheet
fat drinking straw

You can use any shape of hard candy.

1. Mix the sugar and margarine really well, getting rid of any lumps.

2. Mix in half of the beaten egg, a little at a time. You don't need the other half.

3. Sift in the flour and the spice. Mix it really well with a blunt knife.

4. Squeeze the mixture together with your hands to make a firm dough.

5. Roll out the dough on a floury surface until it is ¼ inch thick.

6. Press out large stars. Use a spatula to put them on the cookie sheet.

7. Make a hole in each star by pressing the straw in one of the points.

8. Use the small cutter to cut out a shape in the middle of each star.

Preheat the oven to 350ºF

You could hang the cookies on a Christmas tree or in a window.

. Bake the stars on ıe middle shelf for ve minutes. Take ıem out of the oven.

10. Drop a candy in each middle shape. Be very careful as the sheet will be hot.

11. Bake for five more minutes. Leave the stars on the sheet until they are cold.

12. Thread a thin ribbon through each hole to hang the cookies.

Apricot muffins

For 9 muffins, you will need:

1 cup self-rising flour

$\frac{1}{2}$ cup whole-wheat flour

1 level teaspoon baking powder

1 level teaspoon allspice

$\frac{2}{3}$ cup dried apricots, chopped

$\frac{7}{8}$ cup milk

$\frac{1}{4}$ cup butter, melted

1 large egg

2 teaspoons lemon juice

$\frac{2}{3}$ cup packed, brown sugar

greased muffin tray

1. Sift the self-rising flour. Add the whole-wheat flour and baking powder.

2. Add the spice and apricots. Use a big spoon to mix them in very well.

3. Beat the milk, butter, egg, lemon juice and sugar in another bowl.

4. Use a spoon to make a large hole in the middle of the flour mixture.

You could add maraschino cherries, instead of apricots.

Preheat the oven to 350ºF

5. Pour in half of the beaten mixture. Stir it well. Pour in the rest and mix gently.

6. Put a tablespoon of mix in each hole in the tray. Don't smooth the tops.

7. Bake for about 20-25 minutes, until the tops are golden brown.

You can also make these muffins with chocolate chips, but leave out the spice.

8. Leave the muffins in the tray for five minutes. Put them on a rack to cool.

Flower candy

You will need:
2 cups powdered sugar, sifted
half the white of a small egg, mixed from dried egg white, as directed on the packet
1 tablespoon lemon juice
¼ teaspoon peppermint flavoring
yellow and red food dyes
cookie sheet covered in plastic foodwrap
small flower cookie cutter

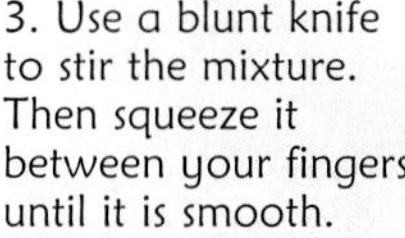

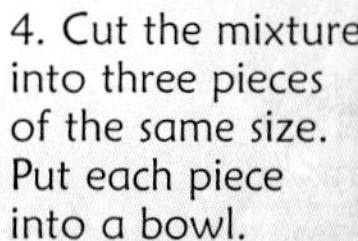

1. Sift the powdered sugar into a deep bowl. Make a hole in the middle of it with a spoon.

2. In a small bowl, mix the egg white, lemon juice and the peppermint. Pour it into the sugar.

3. Use a blunt knife to stir the mixture. Then squeeze it between your fingers until it is smooth.

4. Cut the mixture into three pieces of the same size. Put each piece into a bowl.

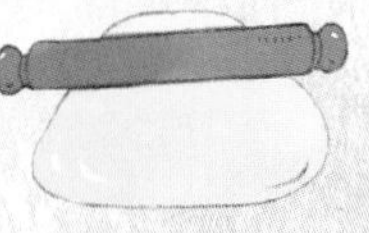

5. Put a few drops of red food dye into one of the bowls. Use a metal spoon to mix it well.

6. Put a few drops of yellow food dye into one of the other bowls. Mix it in very well.

7. Dust powdered sugar over a surface. Roll the yellow mixture until it's as thick as your finger.

8. Use a cookie cutter to cut out as many flowers as you can. Cut them close together.

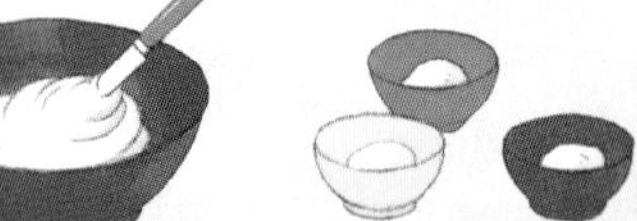

). Use a blunt knife
:o lift the flowers
onto the sheet.
Make red flowers in
the same way.

10. Pull off a piece of white mixture about the size of your thumbnail. Roll it into a ball.

11. Press the ball to flatten it a little then press it into the middle of a flower shape.

2. Make lots
nore white balls
and press them
nto the middles
of the flowers.

13. Leave the flowers on the cookie sheet for at least an hour until they become hard.

Put some candy in a box for a present.

Hot bunnies

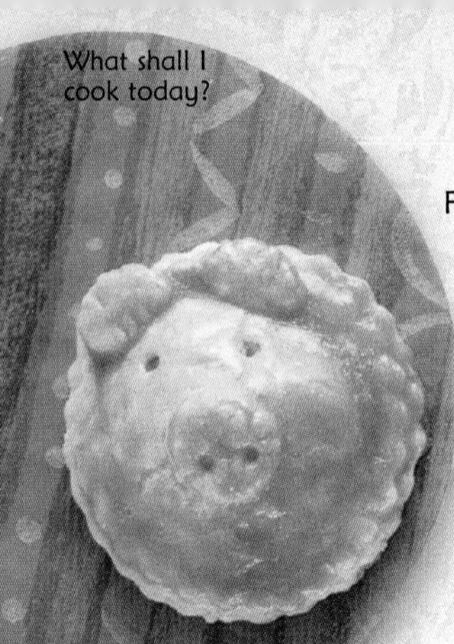

For four bunnies, you will need:
For the pastry:
$1\frac{1}{4}$ cups flour
6 tablespoons margarine
6 teaspoons of very cold water
pinch of salt

For the filling:
$\frac{1}{4}$ cup sausage meat, browned
1 egg, beaten
large, round cookie cutter
bottle top
fat straw
greased cookie sheet

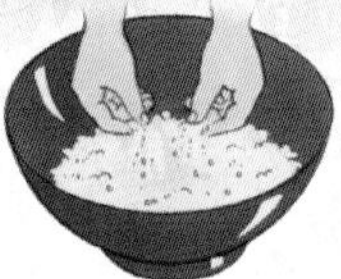

1. To make pastry, mix the flour and salt. Rub in the margarine so that it looks like crumbs.

2. Add the water. Use a blunt knife to mix it in. Squeeze the mixture into a ball of dough.

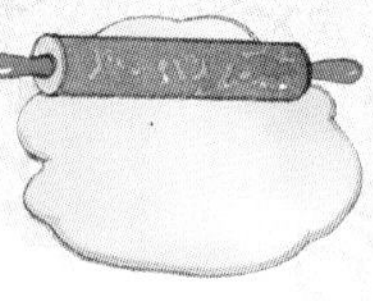

3. Sprinkle some flour onto a work surface. Roll out the pastry until it is flat and thin.

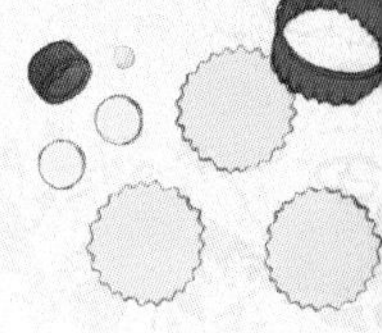

4. Cut twelve circl with the cutter an eight with the bott top. Roll four smal balls for noses.

5. Use a pastry brush to paint one of the large circles with beaten egg.

6. Put a big teaspoon of sausage meat in the middle.

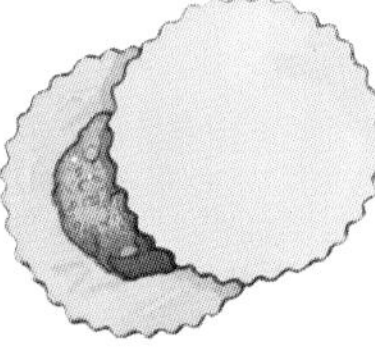

7. Lay one of the big circles on top and flatten it gently with your hand.

8. Press your finge all around the edg Repeat steps 5-8 three more times.

Preheat the oven to 400ºF

9. Brush the tops with egg. Carefully lift them onto the cookie sheet with a spatula.

10. Press on two of the small bottle-top circles for cheeks and a ball for a nose.

11. Cut one ear by pressing the cutter part way across one of the big circles.

To make a pig, cut out the ears and nose with the bottle top. Cut nostrils with a straw.

12. Press the cutter across the other side of the circle to make another ear.

13. Press the ears onto the top. Brush the ears, nose and cheeks with egg.

14. Make two eyes by pushing the end of the straw into the pastry.

15. Bake in the oven for about 15 minutes or until they are golden.

Cheesy snakes and caterpillars

For about eight snakes and four caterpillars, you will need:
1¼ cups self-rising flour
½ teaspoon salt
¼ cup margarine
⅔ cup cheese, finely grated
1 egg and 2 tablespoons of milk, beaten together
raisins for eyes
bottle top
greased cookie sheet

1. Sift the flour and salt. Add the margarine and rub it with your fingers to make crumbs.

2. Leave a tablespoon of cheese on a saucer. Add the rest to the bowl and stir it in.

3. Put a tablespoon of the egg mixture in a cup. Mix the rest into the flour to make dough.

4. Roll out the dough on a floury surface, until it is as thick as your little finger.

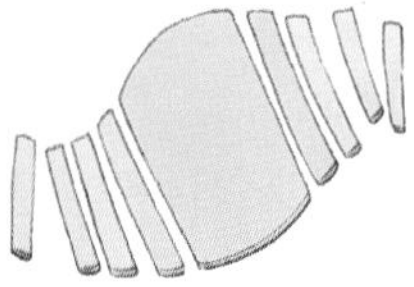

5. Use a blunt knife to cut eight strips as wide as two of your fingers.

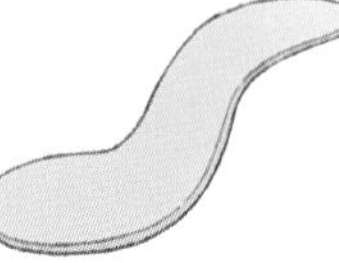

6. Bend the strips into wiggles. Pinch the ends. Press one end flat for a head.

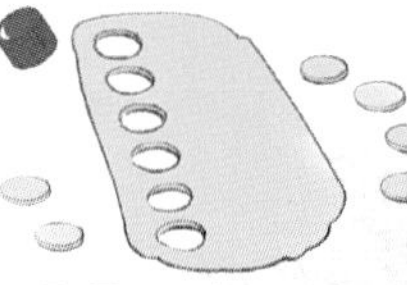

7. To make a caterpillar, cut out six circles of dough with the bottle top.

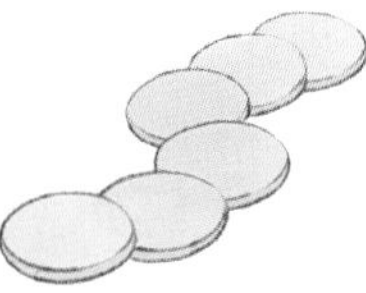

8. Lay the circles in a line. Overlap the edges and press them together.

9. Brush the shapes with the egg mixture. Sprinkle with cheese. Add raisins for eyes.

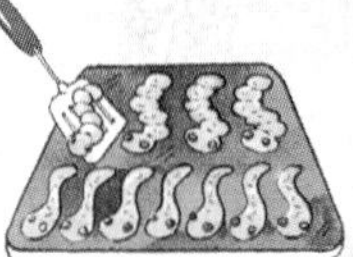

10. Use a spatula to lift the shapes onto the greased cookie sheet.

11. Bake for about eight to ten minutes, until they are golden.

Preheat the oven to 400ºF

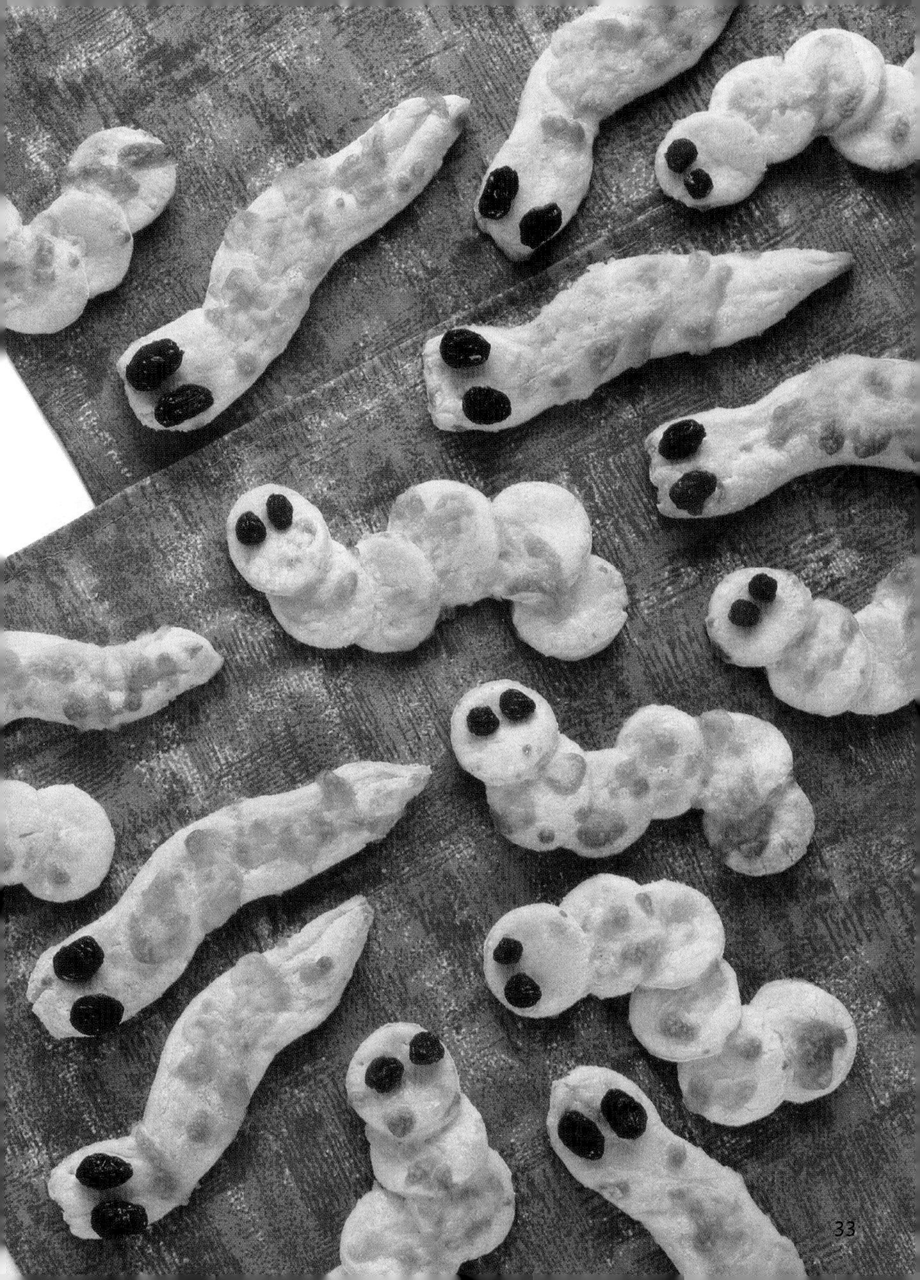

Christmas tree cupcakes

For about 12 cupcakes, you will need:
2 cups all-purpose flour
3 teaspoons baking powder
½ teaspoon salt
½ cup soft margarine
1¼ cups sugar
2 eggs
1 teaspoon vanilla
1 cup milk
paper baking cups
muffin tray
assorted candy

For the butter icing:
¼ cup butter or margarine, softened
2 cups powdered sugar, sifted
green food dye
¼ teaspoon vanilla
2 tablespoons milk

1. Sift the flour, salt and baking powder and add the other cupcake ingredients.

2. Stir everything together until you get a smooth, creamy mixture.

3. Put the baking cups in the muffin tray. Half-fill each one with cake mix.

4. Bake them for about 20 minutes. Leave them on a rack to cool.

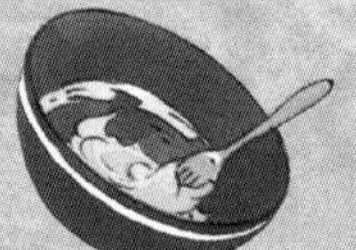

5. To make the butter icing, stir the butter until it is creamy.

6. Stir in some of the powdered sugar. Mix in the rest, a little at a time.

7. Stir in a few drops of the green food dye and the vanilla.

8. Spread icing on top of each cake. Put candy on top to make a pattern.

Preheat the oven to 375ºF

Use bright candy to make different patterns on your cupcakes.

What shall I do today?

Painting

Paint a parrot

1. Paint the body, like this.

2. Make a hand print on either side for the wings.

3. Paint the tail. Add wingtips.

4. Paint the head.

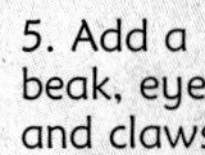

5. Add a beak, eye and claws.

6. Add tips to the wings and tail.

To paint a perching parrot, make a hand print on a slant.

Then paint the rest of the parrot as before.

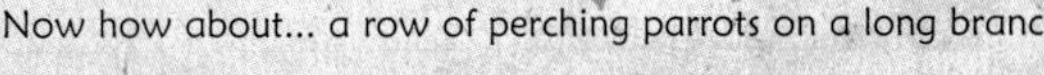

Now how about... a row of perching parrots on a long branch?

To print a leafy background, paint the rough side of a leaf and press it onto the paper.

Paint penguins on the ice

Ice

Sea

Icy sea

1. With a damp cloth, wipe white paint over one end of the paper.

2. In the same way, wipe blue paint over the rest of it.

3. Paint some foodwrap white. Press the painted side over the blue.

4. Lift it off gently and repeat until all the blue is patterne with white.

Penguins

1. Paint a body.

2. Add wings.

3. Let the paint dry.

4. Add a tummy.

Fish

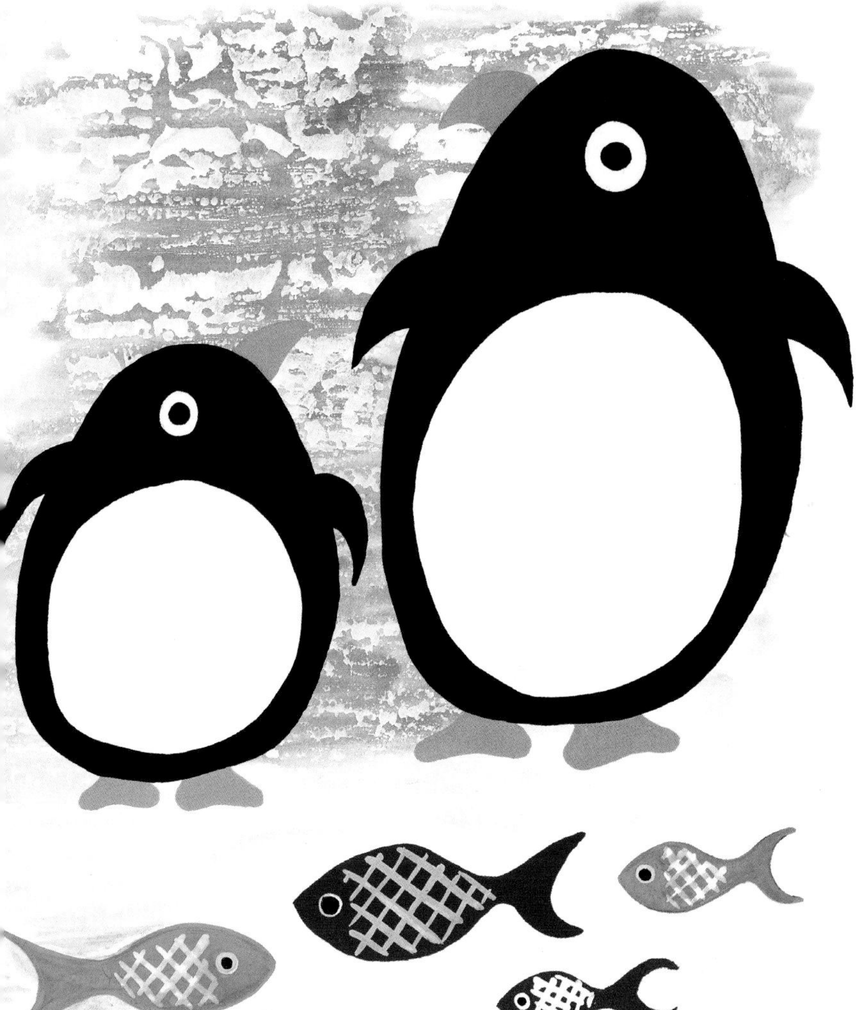

Now how about... ducks on a frozen pond? 

Paint flowers

Poppies

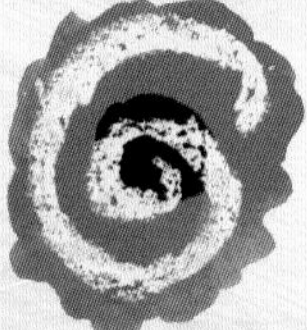

1. Make some swirly petal shapes with a pale candle.
2. Paint over them like this.

Daisies

1. Draw loopy petal shapes with the candle.
2. Paint over them like this.

Tulips

1. Draw upright petal shapes with the candle.
2. Paint over them like this.

Buds

1. Draw small squiggles with the candle.
2. Paint over them like this.

Now how about... a big hat with flowers on it?

Paint a sky picture

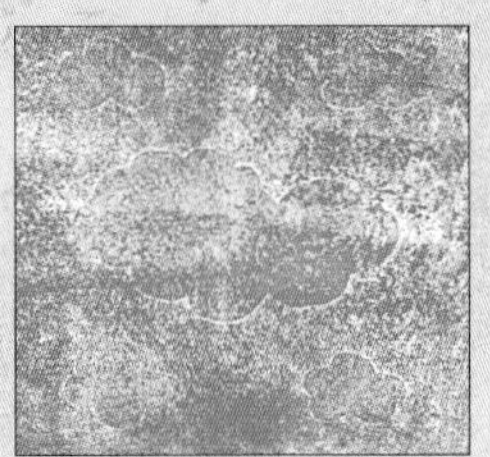

1. Cut cloud shapes out of scrap paper. Lay them on a large sheet of thick paper.

2. With a damp sponge, gently dab blue paint around the edges of all your clouds.

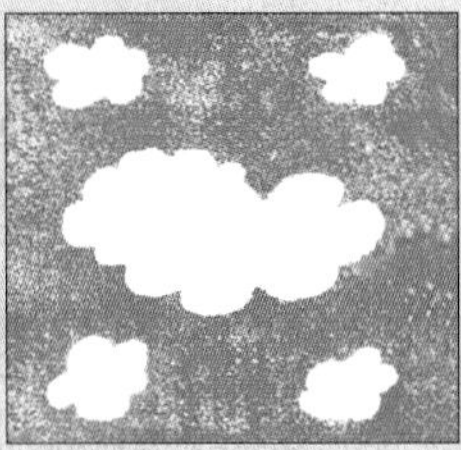

3. When the whole sheet of paper is covered with blue, peel the clouds off gently.

4. Paint some hot-air balloons in the sky. Add some planes doing exciting stunts.

5. When the planes and balloons have dried, decorate them with bright patterns.

6. Add smoke trails to the planes using a piece of damp sponge dipped in paint.

Now how about... kites in the sky?

Paint sheep in a field

1. Draw sheep's bodies and lambs' bodies on pieces of scrap paper. Cut them out.

2. Dip them in water. Shake off the drops, then arrange them on your painting paper.

3. Wind some yarn or wool around an old birthday card. You don't need to wind it very neatly. When the card is covered, tape down the end and cut off the leftover yarn.

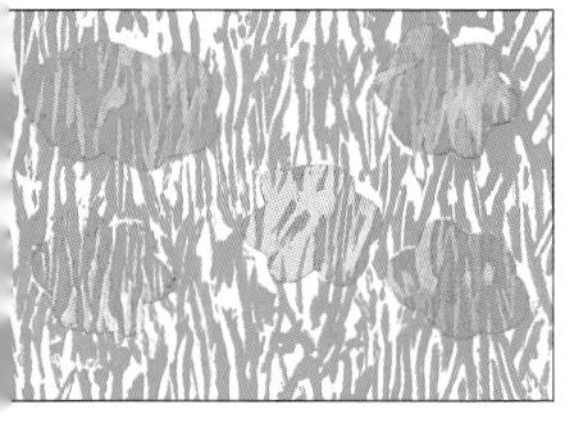

4. Paint the yarn green on one side. Press it all over your paper. Add more paint as you go.

5. Gently peel off the paper sheep. Paint on faces and legs with a fine paintbrush.

6. Add some flowers. Print them with a fingertip.

Now how about... rabbits on a hill?

Paint a face

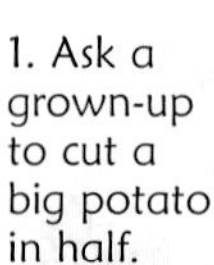

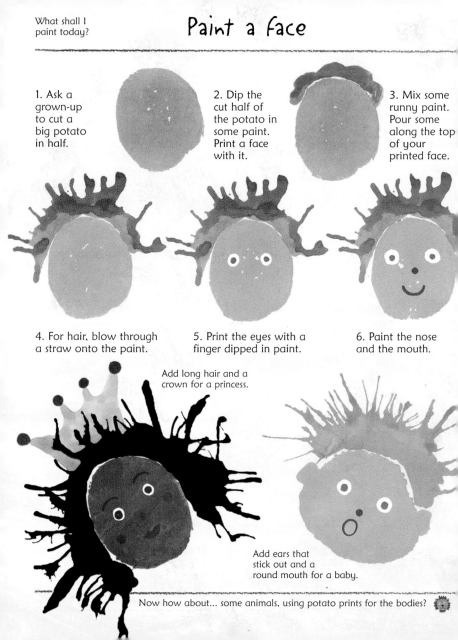

1. Ask a grown-up to cut a big potato in half.

2. Dip the cut half of the potato in some paint. Print a face with it.

3. Mix some runny paint. Pour some along the top of your printed face.

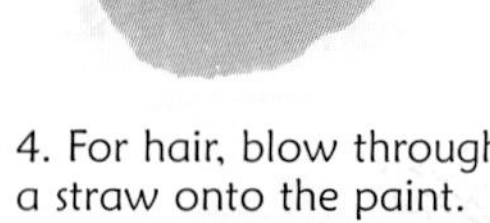

4. For hair, blow through a straw onto the paint.

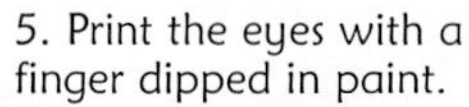

5. Print the eyes with a finger dipped in paint.

6. Paint the nose and the mouth.

Add long hair and a crown for a princess.

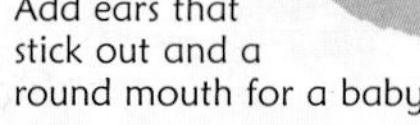

Add ears that stick out and a round mouth for a baby.

Now how about... some animals, using potato prints for the bodies?

For a clown, add bright hair, a red nose and a hat.

You could add a tangly beard as well as hair.

Try adding funny glasses or a bow tie.

Paint fish in a waterfall

1. With a damp cloth, wipe blue stripes down your paper.

2. Add some green stripes to your paper in the same way.

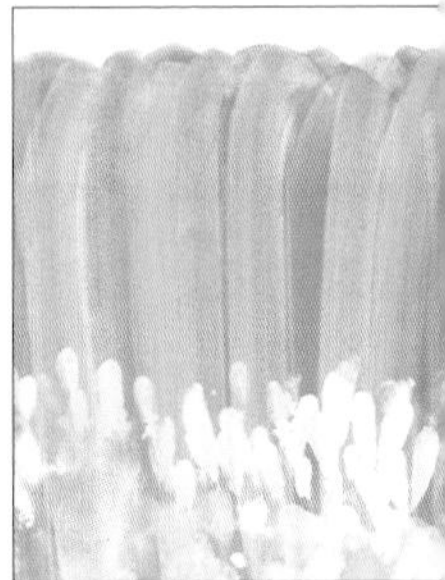

3. Make white handprints along the bottom of your paper.

4. Splash some white paint on with a brush to look like spray.

5. On another piece of paper paint lots of bright fish.

6. Let the paint dry. Add patterns on top.

7. Cut the fish out. Glue them onto the waterfall picture.

Now how about... an underwater picture with handprints for seaweed?

What shall I do today?

Gardening

Grow sprout shapes

1. Tear off ten paper towels. Lay them on a large flat plate or a small plastic tray.

2. Use a spoon to put water on the paper towels. Add water until they are soaking.

3. Lay some cookie cutters on the towels with their sharp edges pointing down.

4. Use a teaspoon to sprinkle lots of alfalfa seeds into each shape. Do this carefully.

You can eat the alfalfa you have grown. Try it in an egg sandwich or a salad.

You can grow these at any time. They will grow in 4-5 days.

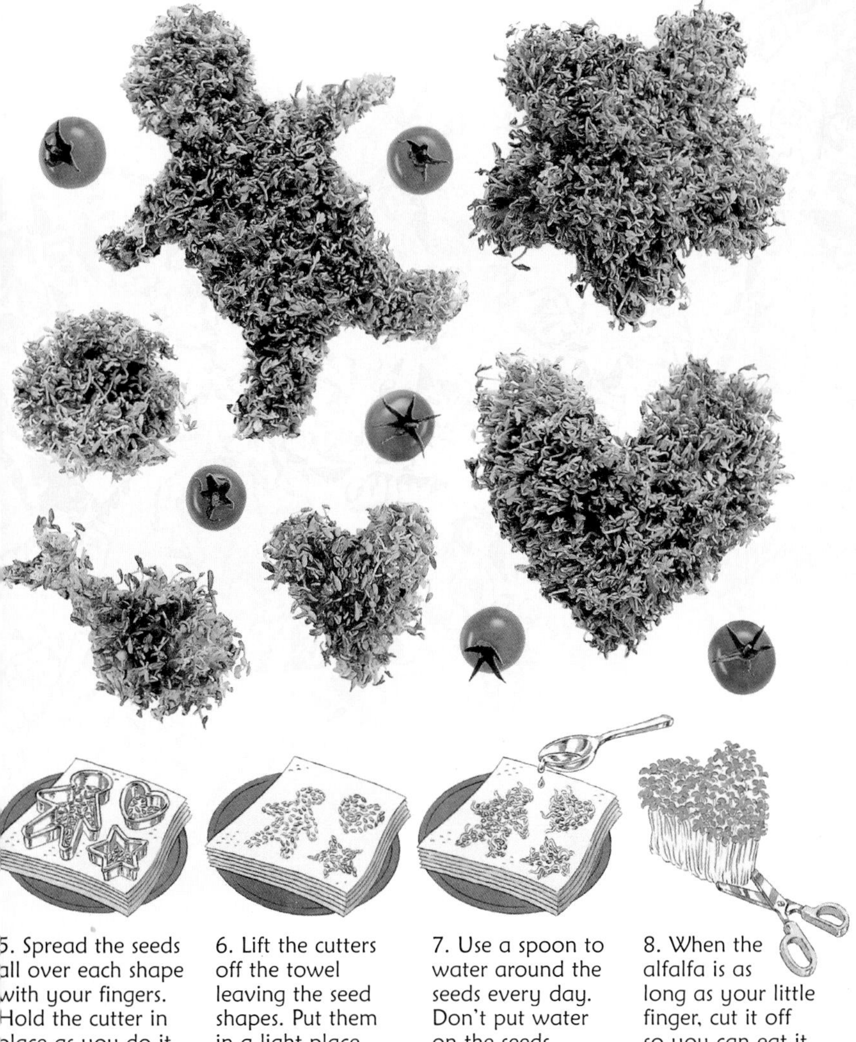

5. Spread the seeds all over each shape with your fingers. Hold the cutter in place as you do it.

6. Lift the cutters off the towel leaving the seed shapes. Put them in a light place.

7. Use a spoon to water around the seeds every day. Don't put water on the seeds.

8. When the alfalfa is as long as your little finger, cut it off so you can eat it.

Grow roots and shoots

1. Soak a big jar in warm water and peel off its labels so you can see inside.

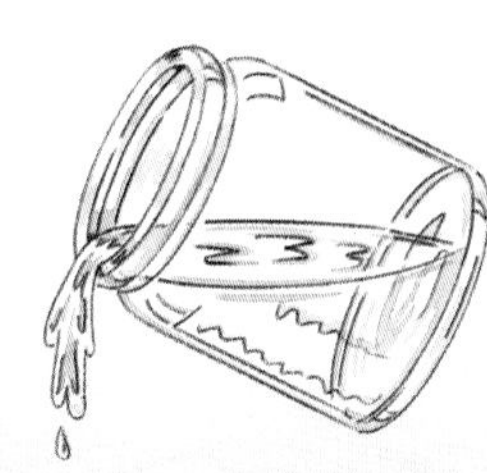

2. Rinse the inside of the jar with cold water. Empty it out but don't dry it.

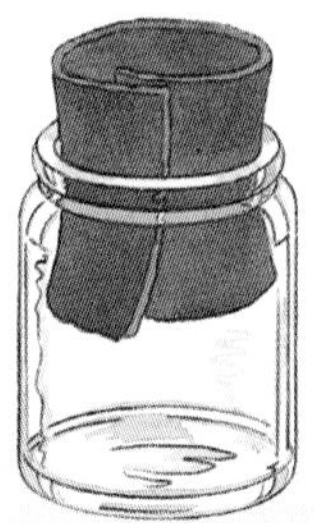

3. Fold a paper napkin in half. Curl it into a circle and slip it inside the jar.

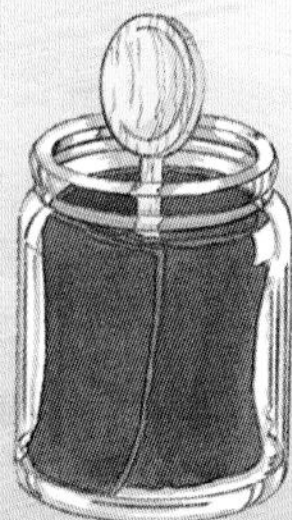

4. Press the napkin against the side of the jar with the handle of a spoon.

5. Peel back part of the napkin. Push a lima bean in against the jar.

You can grow these at any time. They take 2-3 weeks.

The roots will start to grow first, then the shoots.

6. Add two more beans around the jar. Wet the napkin with lots of water.

7. Put the jar in a bright, warm place. Add water often to keep the napkin wet.

Grow leafy stems

1. You need a pot or a mug and some florist's foam (the kind that's used to arrange flowers in a basket or vase).

2. Soak the foam in a bowl of water. Leave it in the water until bubbles stop coming to the surface.

3. Push the foam into your pot. Use scissors to trim it so that it is a little bit below the top of the pot.

4. Ask if you can cut pieces from plants which have woody stems. Make them just longer than your hand.

5. The pieces you have cut are called cuttings. Snip a straight end just below a leaf of each cutting.

6. Pull off the bottom leaves. Push the end of the stem into the foam near to the edge.

7. Arrange your cuttings around the edge of the pot. Push them in well so they don't fall out.

8. Put your pot on a windowsill but out of very bright sunshine. Water the foam often to keep it damp.

9. When new leaves grow, take the foam out of the pot and look to see if roots have grown.

10. Take a blunt knife and carefully cut the foam away from each cutting. Try not to damage their roots.

11. Plant each cutting in a pot full of potting soil. Water it and put it outside in a warm, light place.

Do this in fall. They will grow in 6-8 weeks.

When you plant your cuttings, make sure that you don't forget to water them.
Cuttings in foam
Rosemary
Box
Sage
You can plant more than one ivy cutting in a pot.
Lavender
Ivy

Grow a leaf into a plant

1. Fill a small bottle with water. Don't fill it quite to the top, so that you leave a small space.

2. Cut a paper square and fasten it over the top of the bottle with a rubber band.

3. Use scissors to cut a leaf with its stalk from an African violet plant.

4. The leaf should be from near the outside and should look healthy.

Leave your plant in a light place, but not on a very sunny windowsill.

5. Hold the bottle. Make a hole in the middle of the paper with a very sharp pencil.

6. Push the stalk through the hole. Its end should go in the water. Add more water if you need to.

7. After a few days, tiny roots and new leaves will appear. It is now ready to plant in a pot.

8. Make a hole in some soil. Put the plant in it and gently press around it. Water your plant.

Put your pot on a saucer. When you water it, pour the water into the saucer, not on the plant.

Grow herbs on a windowsill

1. Buy some fresh herbs which are growing in a pot from a supermarket.

2. Wash out some empty one pint milk cartons. You will need one for each herb.

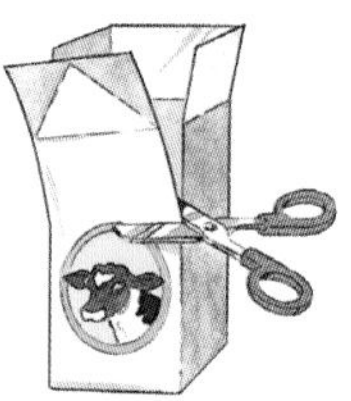

3. Dry the cartons. Snip halfway down one side. Then cut the top off all the way around.

4. Turn each carton over. Make a hole in the bottom with the point of a sharp pencil.

5. Put some stones into the bottom of each carton. Spoon in a little potting soil.

6. Take each herb out of its pot by tipping it over and tapping the bottom of the pot.

Grow them at any time of the year. They will grow for 4-8 weeks.

7. Fill the gap between the carton and the roots with soil. Press the top of the soil.

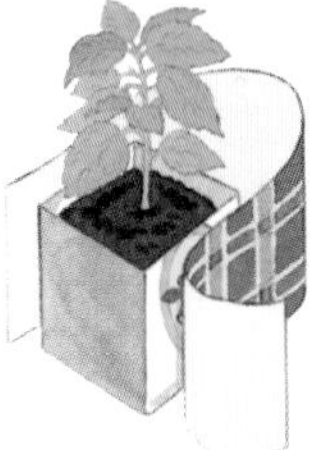

8. Cut a strip of paper long enough to go around and slightly wider than each carton.

9. Wrap one of the pieces of paper carefully around each carton. Tape it at the back.

10. Put your herbs onto a tray and leave them on a windowsill. Keep the soil moist.

Parsley

Basil

Thyme

Grow an ivy tower

1. Put stones into a very large pot which has a hole in it. Fill it with potting soil.

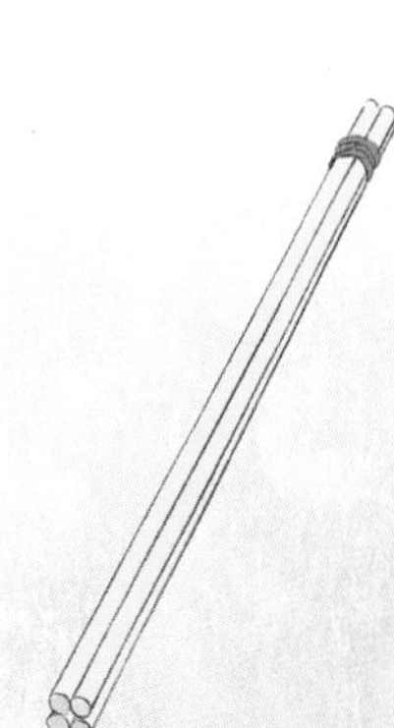

2. Use a rubber band to fasten four short garden canes together near to one end, like this.

3. Spread out the canes. Push them well into the pot, with their ends nearly touching the sides.

4. Dig a small hol at the bottom of one of the canes. Put an ivy plant into the hole.

5. Add a little soil around the plant and press it down firmly with your knuckles.

6. Dig a hole at the bottom of the other three canes. Plant an ivy in each hole.

7. Hold the longest stem of each plant and twist it carefully around its cane. Water your plants.

8. As the ivy grows, twist each stem around its cane every two or three days.

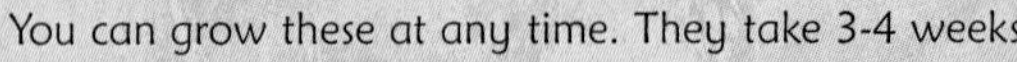

You can grow these at any time. They take 3-4 weeks.

Paint your pot with acrylic paint and put lots of Christmas decorations on your ivy tower.

Grow tiny islands in the sea

1. Cut the top off some vegetables which have sprouted a little. Cut them as thick as this.

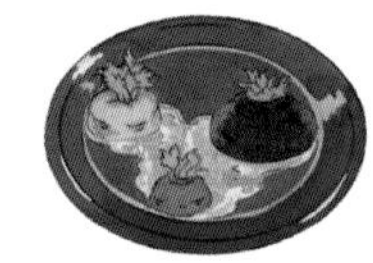

2. Put a little cold water into a shallow dish. Spread the vegetable tops over the bottom.

3. Carefully pour in a little more water around the vegetable tops but don't cover them.

4. Put the dish on a windowsill. Add a little water each day. The shoots wil grow in a few days

Use vegetables such as carrots, parsnips, turnips and beets.

Your shoots should grow to look like tall trees on islands.

You can grow these at any time

Grow a moss garden

1. Put a thin layer of potting soil into the bottom of a shallow tray, with no holes in the bottom of it.

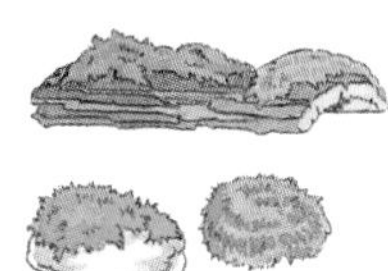

2. Hunt for some moss on lawns, walls and between paving slabs. Look on stones and pieces of bark too.

3. Dig up small pieces of moss and put them on your tray. Add mossy stones and pieces of bark.

4. Collect some rainwater if you can, but tap water will do, and spray the moss well every day.

Watch your mosses grow.

Add some shells too.

row at any time.

What shall I do
today?
Making things

Make a furry snake

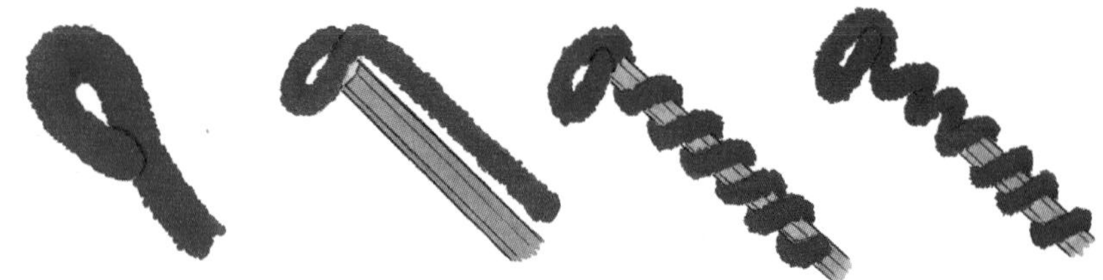

1. For the head, bend over one end of a pipecleaner.

2. Put it along a pencil and bend the head over the end.

3. Wind the long end around and around the pencil.

4. Gently pull the snake halfway off the pencil.

5. Cut some paper eyes and glue them onto the head.

6. Draw a red tongue. Cut it out and glue it on.

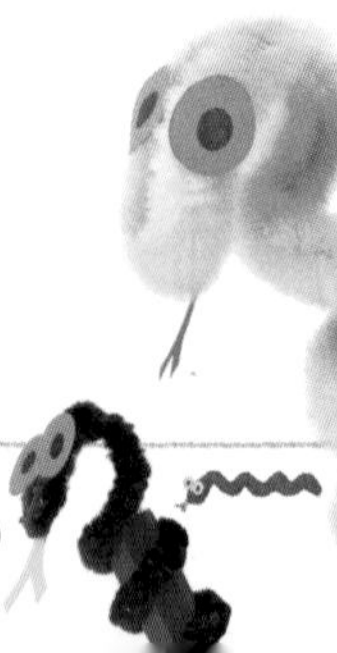

Make twisted bangles

1. Take two pencils and tape them together like this.

2. Lay two pipecleaners side by side. Twist them together at one end.

3. Put the pencils between the pipecleaners, close to the twisted part.

4. Twist the pipecleaners tightly next to the pencils, three times.

5. Pull out the pencils. Put them in between the pipecleaners and twist.

6. Keep on doing this to the end. Press the twisted pipecleaners flat.

7. Bend them into a circle. Twist the ends together.

Make bread shapes

These bread shapes are decorations only. Do not eat them.

1. Press a big cookie cutter firmly into a slice of white bread.

2. Push the shape gently out of the cutter.

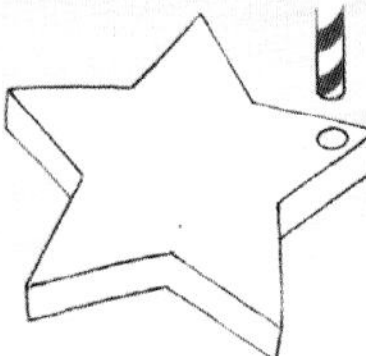

3. Make a hole by pressing the end of a straw into the shape.

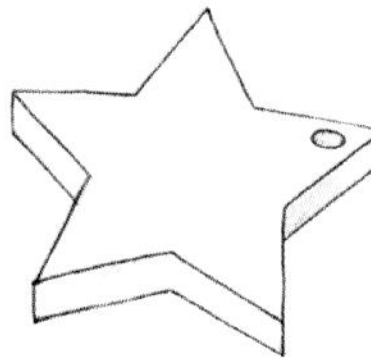

4. Put it onto a cooling rack and leave it overnight to go hard.

5. Mix a little paint with household glue (PVA). Paint the edges of the shape.

6. Paint the top. When it is dry, turn it over and paint the other side.

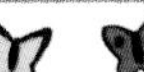

7. Glue on lots of glitter, sequins or beads to decorate your shape.

8. Push some thread through the hole. Bring the ends together to make a loop.

9. Push the ends of the thread through the loop to make a knot.

Make paper flowers

A daisy

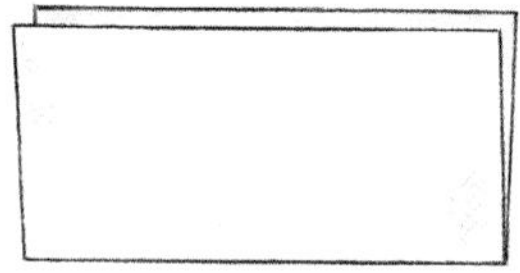

1. Fold a sheet of kitchen paper towel in half. Open it out. Cut along the fold.

2. Fold one piece in half, long sides together. You don't need the other piece.

3. Draw lots of stripes along the paper with a felt-tip pen.

4. Fold the paper in half with the short sides together, then fold it in half again.

5. Make long cuts close together from the bottom. Don't cut all the way up.

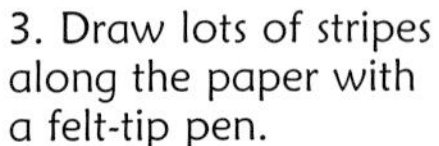

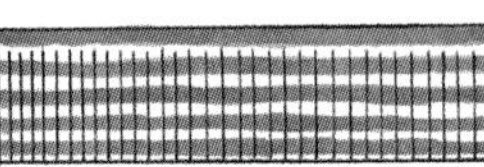

6. Open it carefully, so that it looks like this.

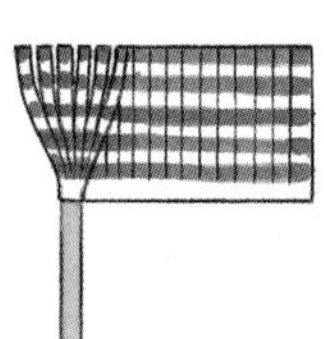

7. Tape one end of the paper onto a bendable straw. Roll the paper tightly around it.

8. Fasten the loose end with tape. Pull all the petals down.

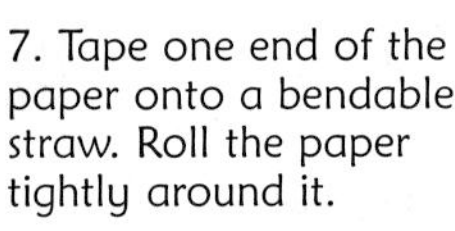

9. Snip little pieces of yellow paper or yarn. Glue them into the middle.

You can use tissue paper for bright flowers. Cut the paper the same size as a piece of paper towel.

Another flower

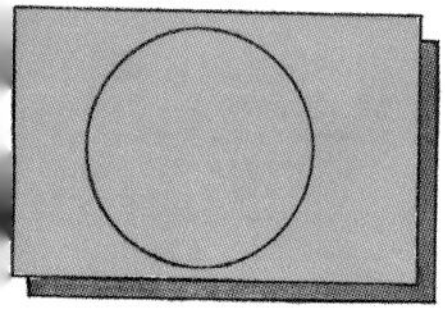

1. Take two sheets of tissue paper. Put a small plate or saucer on top and draw around it.

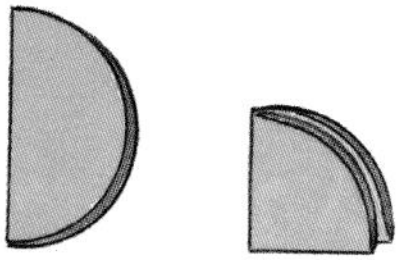

2. Cut around the circle through both layers of tissue paper. Fold them in half and in half again.

3. Twist the corner and tape it onto the end of a straw. Gently pull the petals apart.

4. Make a ball of tissue paper and glue it in the middle.

Make a fish

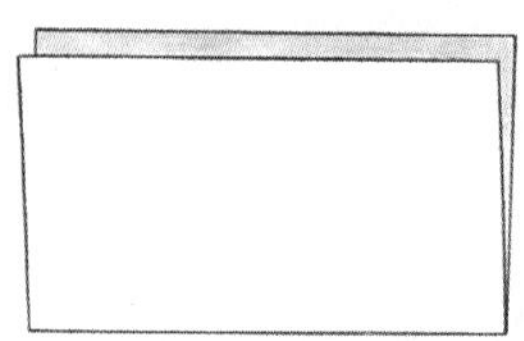

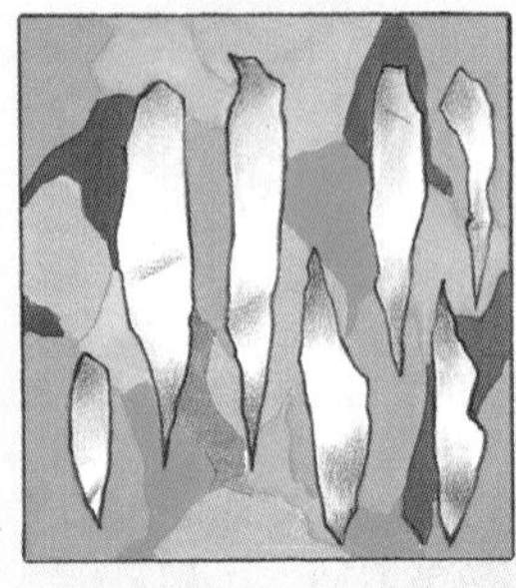

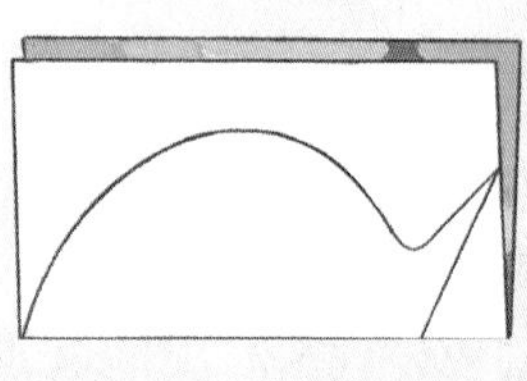

1. Fold a piece of paper in half, long sides together. Open it. Crease it back along the same fold.

2. Open the paper. Tear pieces of tissue paper. Glue them on. Add lots of strips of kitchen foil.

3. Fold the paper in half. Crease the fold well. Draw half a fat fish shape. Cut it out.

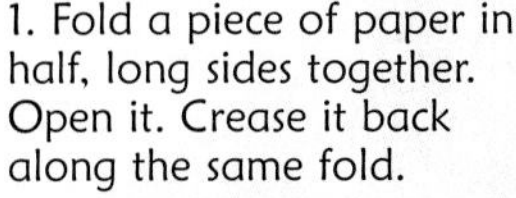

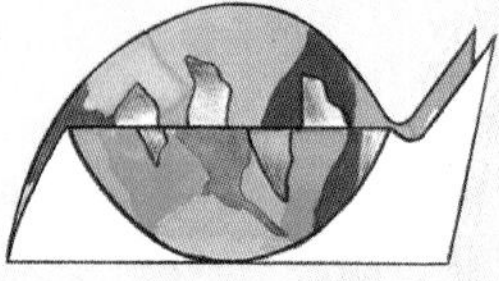

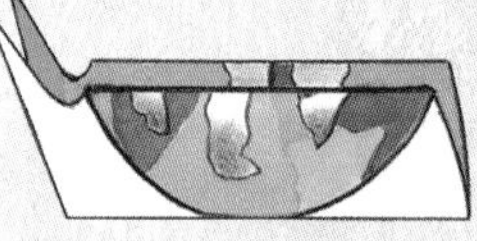

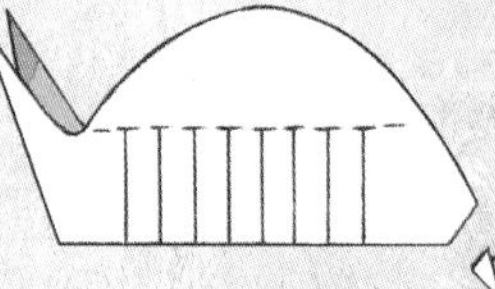

4. Bend over one of the top edges until it touches the fold at the bottom. Press hard to crease it.

5. Turn the fish over. Bend the other top edge over in the same way. Remember to crease it well.

6. Unfold the top pieces. Snip a mouth. Make cuts as wide as your finger, up to the fold.

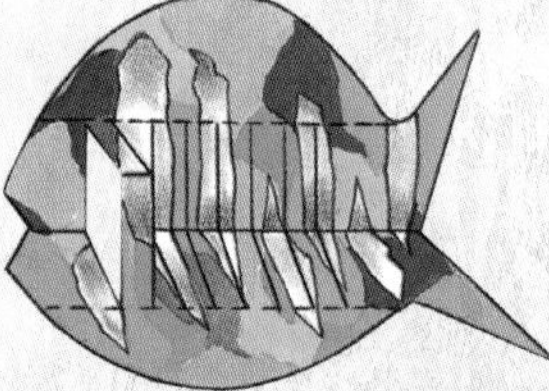

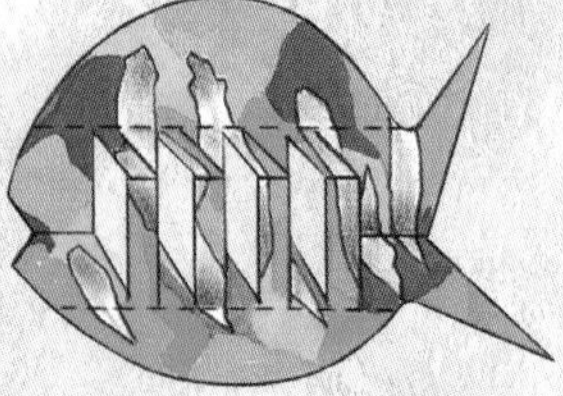

7. Half open the fish. Hold the head and pull the first strip out. Pinch the fold in the middle so that it stands up.

8. Skip the next strip. Pull out the next one. Go on in the same way until you reach the last strip. Pinch all the folds well.

Use bright thread to hang up your fish.

Make a crown

1. Cut a band of stiff paper to fit around your head, plus a little bit.

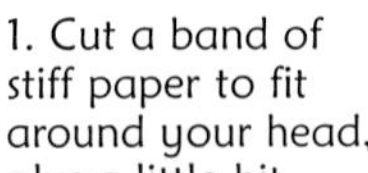

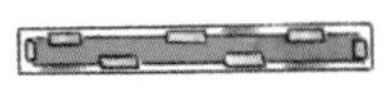

2. Lay it on a bigger piece of kitchen foil. Fold the foil edges in and tape them down.

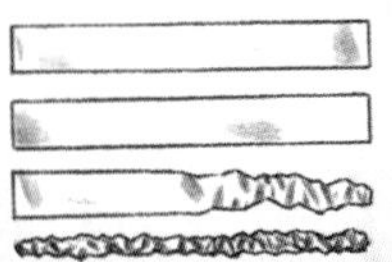

3. Cut four strips of foil as wide as the band. Squeeze them to make thin sticks.

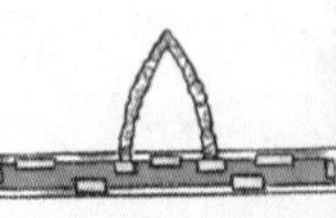

4. Bend one in half. Tape it onto the middle of the band, at the back

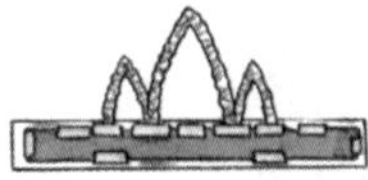

5. Cut a little from the end of two pieces. Bend them and tape them on.

6. Cut the last piece in half. Bend each piece. Tape them on at each end.

7. Cut shiny shapes. Tape them on so you can see them above the band.

8. Turn the band over. Glue on scraps of bright paper or foil.

For an icy crown, use only blue and silver paper.

Make a smaller crown for a ballerina.

9. Tape the ends of the crown together to fit around your head.

For a king's crown, glue cotton balls around the bottom. Add spots with a felt-tip pen for a fur effect.

Make a lacy card

1. Draw some leaves, flowers and hearts on thick white paper.

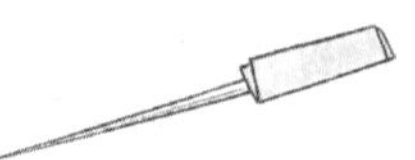

2. Wrap sticky tape around the end of a darning needle to make a handle. Lay several kitchen paper towels over a folded newspaper. Put your drawing on top.

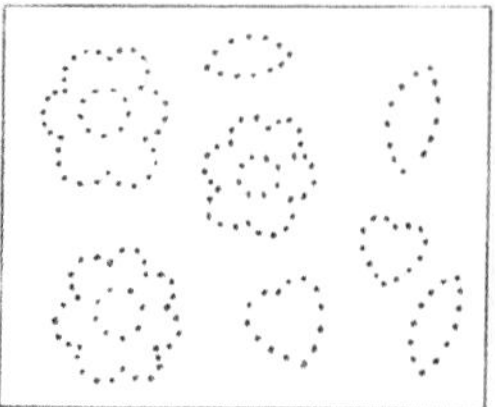

3. Use the needle to prick around the shapes. Press quite hard.

4. Cut around all the shapes very carefully. Leave a narrow edge around the holes.

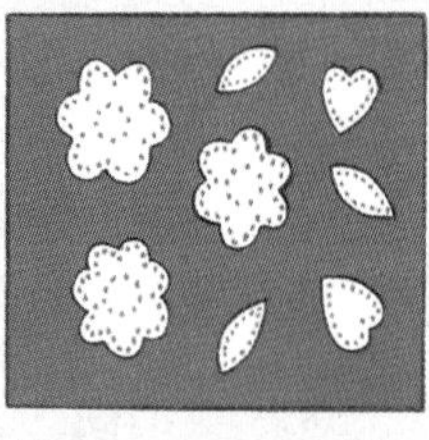

5. Dab glue stick on the pencil side of each shape. Press them very gently onto thin cardboard.

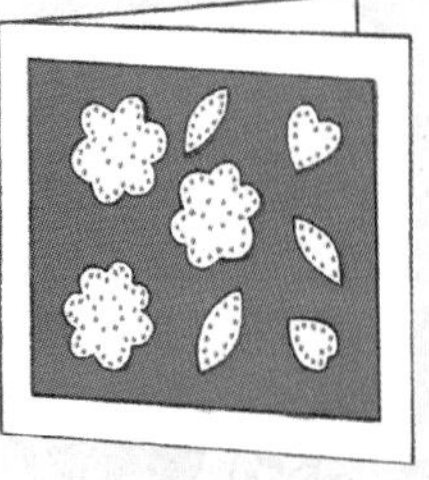

6. To make a card, glue your picture onto a slightly bigger piece of folded cardboard.

Make stamps

Draw a stamp and prick around the edges. Tear it carefully along the holes.

You don't need to use white paper for all your shapes.

Prick a wavy line around your shape. Cut around it, but leave a narrow edge.

What shall I do today?

Dressing up

A scarecrow

1. Tape lots of clean dry straw or long grass inside an old hat.

2. Sponge brown face paint in patches on your face. Sponge red on your cheeks.

3. Brush on spiked eyebrows and a mustache with brown face paint.

4. Dab face paint on your nose and add big freckles. Brush red on your lips too.

5. Pull on a big plaid shirt and some old pants or a skirt.

6. Put on some old boots or shoes. Put rubber bands around your ankles.

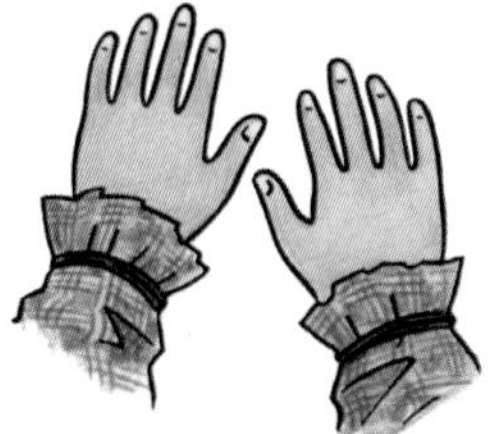

7. Put rubber bands around your wrists. Don't make them tight.

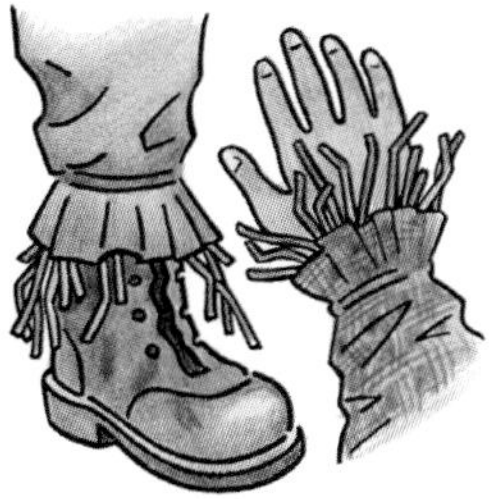

3. Push straw into your cuffs and pant legs, under the rubber bands.

Tie a bright scarf around your neck and pin a toy mouse to your hat.

Put a belt around your waist and push straw under it.

A puppy

1. If your hair is short, tie a ribbon or a piece of elastic around your head.

2. Stuff a pair of short socks with lots of cotton balls to make the ears.

3. Tuck the socks into the band. Use bobby pins to hold them in place.

4. Dab white face paint over your face. Close your eyes when you get near them.

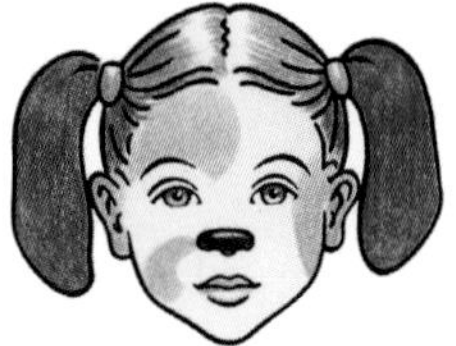

5. Dab orange face paint on in patches. Brush black on the end of your nose.

6. Use a brush and brown face paint to add spots and big patches.

7. Brush a black line from your nose to your top lip. Brush along your lip too.

8. Add a red tongue on your bottom lip. Add dots on either side of your nose.

Long hair

1. If your hair is long, tie it into two high bunches.

2. Push each bunch into a short sock. Fasten them with bands.

   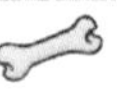  

After you have painted your face, put socks on your hands and feet, for paws.

A lucky pirate

1. Sponge light brown face paint over your face.

2. Brush on big eyebrows and a curly mustache.

3. Dab stubble on your chin with a toothbrush.

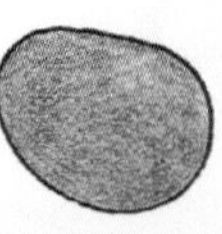

4. Cut out an eyepatch shape fro stiff black paper.

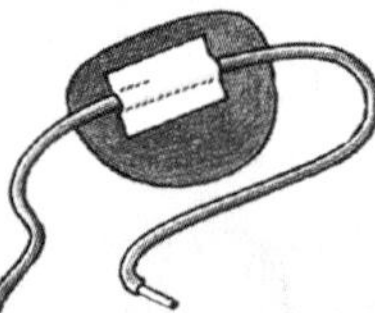

5. Tape a shoelace across the back of the eyepatch, near to the top.

6. Get someone to tie the eyepatch and knot a scarf around your head.

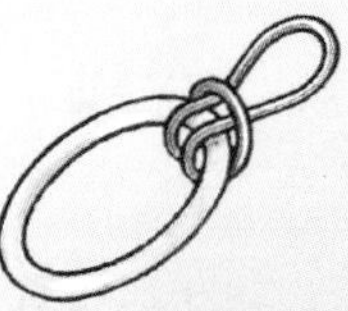

7. Slip a rubber band through a curtain ring. Hang it over your ear.

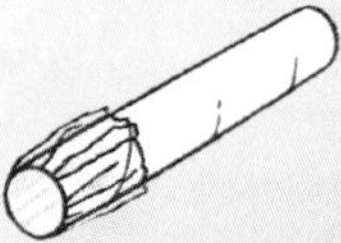

8. For a telescope, paint a cardboard tube. Put foodwrap over one end.

Use face paint to make a scar on your cheek.

Put some old necklaces and brooches in your treasure box too.

Make a treasure box

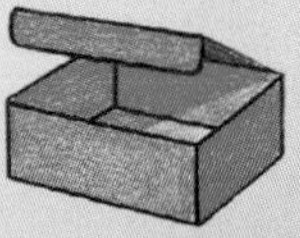

Find a box with a lid, like a chocolate or teabag box. Paint it.

Cover things like bottle tops and cookies with foil to make treasure.

You could safety-pin a toy parrot on your shoulder.

'ou can face aint a curly eard instead f stubble.

Wear a leather belt across one shoulder.

A spotted bug

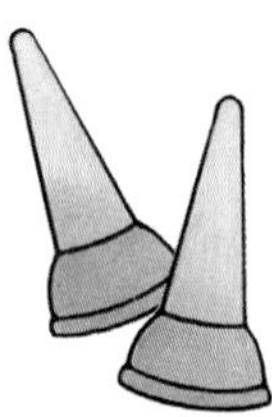

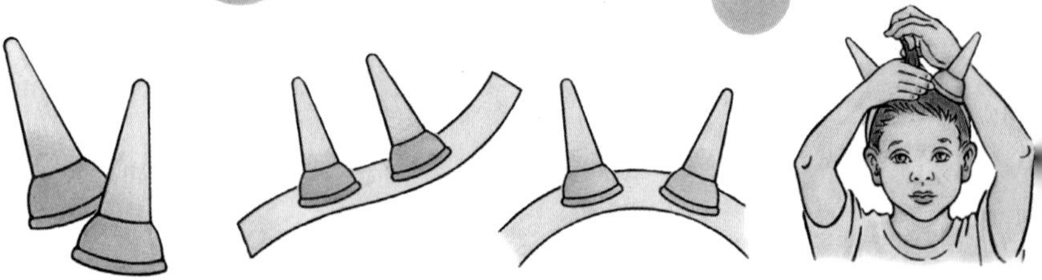

1. Put two ice-cream cones on newspaper. Paint them then leave them to dry.

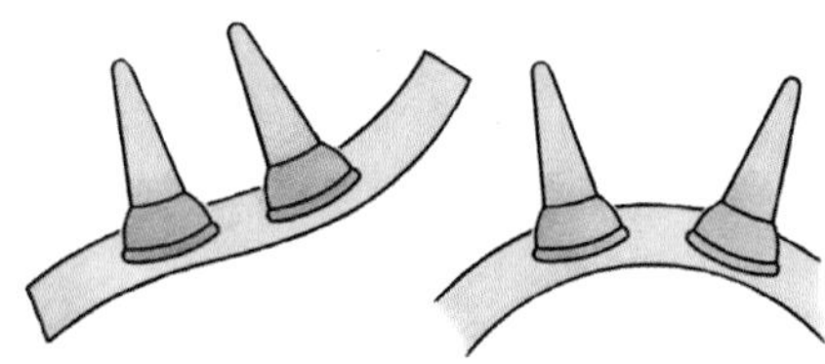

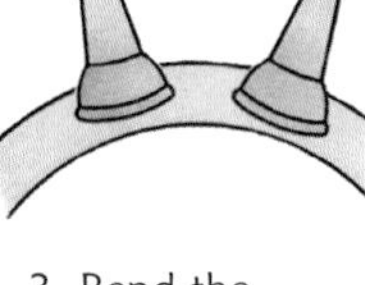

2. Cut a strip of thin cardboard to fit over the top of your head. Glue the cones onto it.

3. Bend the cardboard around your head. Fasten it at each side with bobby pins.

4. Put a blob of ha
gel onto your hanc
Lift up a big clump
of your hair in you
other hand.

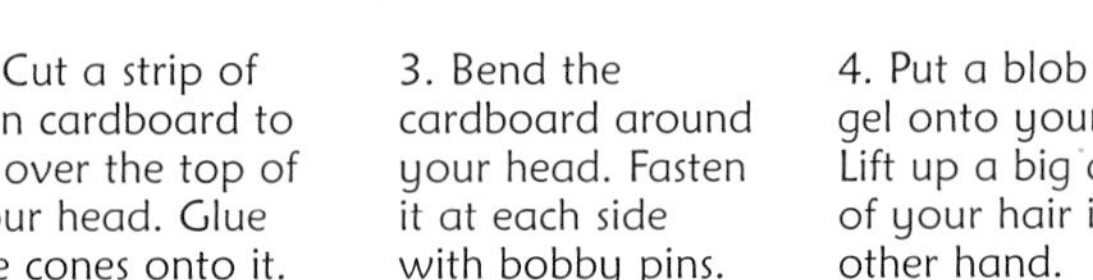

Remember you can't eat the cones once they are painted.

5. Squeeze your gelled hand around a clump of hair and pull it up. Do this to more clumps of hair.

6. Rub a damp sponge in face paint. Dab it over your face. Leave gaps for spots.

7. Use a brush and a different face paint to draw the outlines of spots in the gaps.

8. Fill in the spots with a brush. Close your eye when you fill in any spots that are near it.

Put face paint on your hands and arms.

Cut out spots and tape them onto a bright T-shirt.

A chef on TV

Make a chef's hat

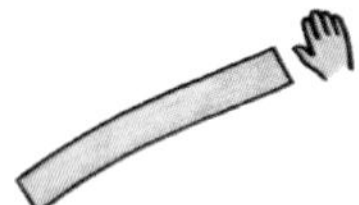

1. Cut a strip of white cardboard as tall as your hand and which fits around your head.

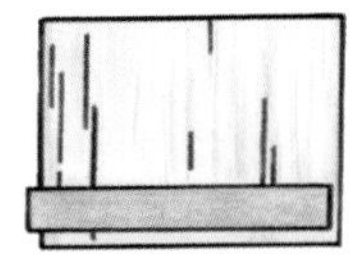

2. Cut a piece of white crêpe paper so it is the same length as the cardboard.

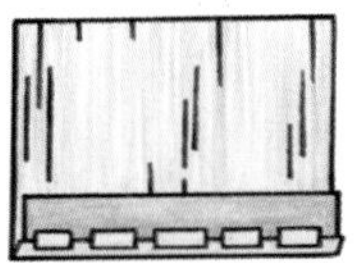

3. Lay the cardboard near the bottom of the paper. Fold the bottom edge over and tape it in place.

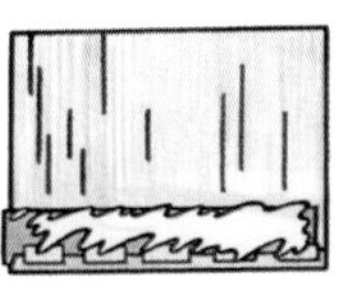

4. Put glue on the cardboard. Fold the cardboard over onto the crêpe paper and press it flat.

5. Hold the paper at each side. Pull your hands apart gently to stretch the paper like this.

6. Bend the cardboard around your head. Use small pieces of tape to join the ends.

7. Gather the top edge of the paper together and wrap a rubber band around it.

8. Press down the top of your hat so that it is flat on top. Puff it out around the sides.

Joke sausages

1. Carefully cut one leg from an old pair of pink or brown tights.

2. Squeeze four sheets of toilet paper to make a sausage shape.

3. Roll four pieces of paper around the sausage. Push it into the tights.

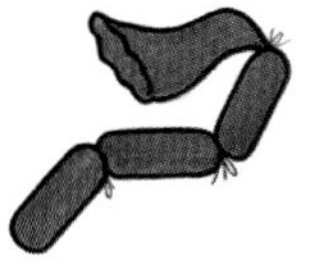

4. Tie thread at the end of the sausage. Make more sausages the same way.

Dressing up

Brush on a mustache with face paint. Add a little beard.

Put on an apron. Dip your fingers in flour and dab them over the apron.

Act as if you are doing a television show about cooking.
Dab some flour on your nose.
Collect some bowls, pans and spoons from your kitchen. Put them on a table in front of you.

Cinderella

Pull some wispy pieces from cotton balls and put them in your hair, as cobwebs.

Before

1. Cut the bottom of an old skirt into rags. Sew or use safety pins to add bright patches.

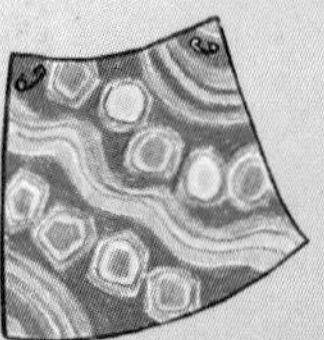

2. Use a safety pin to fasten a piece of bright material around your waist as an apron.

3. Fold a scarf like this. Wrap it around your shoulders and knot the ends in front of you.

4. Sponge some pink face paint on your cheeks. Add some gray for dirty patches.

Make a broom

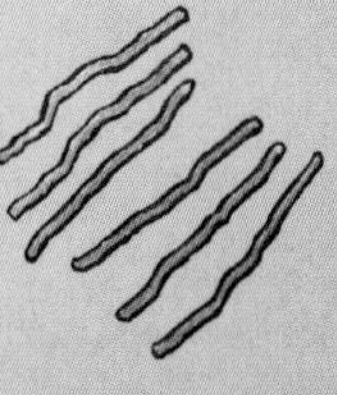

1. Collect lots of thin twigs. Snap them so that they are all about the same length.

2. Make them into a bunch around a stick. Wrap string around and around then tie it.

After

1. Put on some pale tights and a pretty undershirt, leotard or swimsuit.

2. Tie some elastic around your waist. Tuck a piece of lace into it for a skirt.

3. Tie a strip of material or a piece of ribbon around your waist to hide the elastic.

4. For gloves, cut half way down the legs of some old lacy tights. Cut the toes off too.

Paint your face

1. Dip a paintbrush in red face paint. Brush red flowers on your forehead and on your cheeks.

2. Brush a bow near each eyebrow and wavy lines between the flowers. Add green leaves too.

Tie bows on your shoulders and in your hair.

Make a fan by folding up a piece of gift wrap.

Glue fake flowers to your skirt.

Face painting

You can use face painting crayons, but the face paints which look like a box of paints are the best to use.

1. Make sure that your face is clean and dry. Put on the dressing-up clothes you are going to wear.

2. Wrap a towel around your neck to protect your clothes. Tie your hair back or put on a hairband.

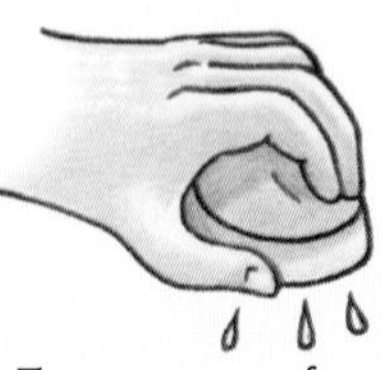

3. To cover your face in paint, dip a sponge in water then squeeze it until no more water comes out.

4. Rub the sponge in the face paint. Dab it all over your face and over your eyelids and lips.

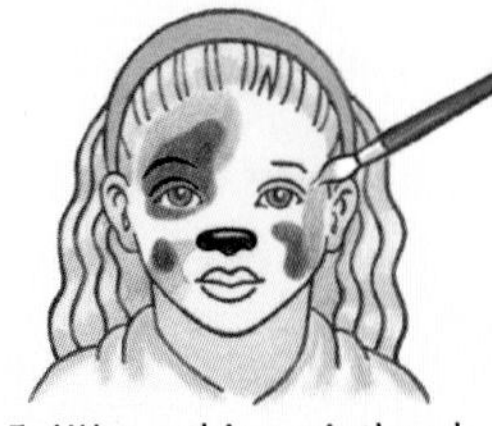

5. Wet a thin paintbrush and rub it in a face paint. Draw on the patterns with the tip of the brush.

A spotted bug

A puppy